D0660501

Elizabeth Gail

THE
DISAPPEARANCE

3

HILDA STAHL

Tyndale House Publishers, Inc.
Wheaton, Illinois

TYNDALE
KIDS

Dedicated with love to
Ron, Donna, Matt, and Sarah

CONTENTS

❁ ❁ ❁

Snowball Disappears

"SHE'S gone!" Elizabeth Gail Dobbs rushed into the house, slamming the door behind her. "Mom, Snowball's gone! We gotta find her!"

Vera jumped up from the piano bench and took hold of Libby's arms. "What? What's wrong, Libby? Calm down!"

"Oh, Mom, Snowball is gone!" Libby cried. "We looked everywhere and she's gone!" Hot tears stung her eyes. Her heart felt as if it might leap through her jacket.

Vera pulled Libby close for a quick hug, then released her. "A white filly can't be that hard to find. She was in the barn this morning with the other horses when I let them out into the pen. Did you see if the fence was down?"

"Ben's checking now. Susan, Kevin, and Toby are looking around the farm in different places." Libby frantically grabbed Vera's hand. "If Snowball gets on the road, she might get hit by a car." Libby tugged Vera's hand. "We've got to find her now!"

"We will, honey. Don't worry." Vera slipped on her blue spring jacket and zipped it up. She wrapped a scarf around her head and followed Libby out into the brisk air. "Hop in the car, Libby," she said. "I'll drive up and down the road, and you watch out for Snowball. A white filly should be easy to spot on a gray, gloomy day like today."

Libby forced herself to sit still in the car as Vera drove slowly down the road. Libby wanted to run instead of ride. The car felt stuffy to her after being out in the cool, damp air.

As they drove past the Wilkens place, Libby saw Joe batting a ball in the front yard. Vera stopped the car and Libby rolled down her window. A blast of wind whipped her short hair back. "Joe, have you seen Snowball? She isn't in the barn or the pen."

Joe dropped his bat and ball and ran to the car. His nose and ears were red from the cold. "I haven't seen her, Libby, but I'll help you

2

look. Maybe she's on the state property behind our fence line."

"We'll let you know if we find her," said Vera as she eased the car off the shoulder and back onto the road. She drove slowly along the road, turned around at the mile crossroad, and drove back toward home.

Libby blinked back tears when she saw that Snowball wasn't back in the pen. She was glad when Vera drove past their driveway and continued down the road. Soon they stopped in Grandma Feuder's driveway.

"Libby, go ask Grandma if she's seen Snowball." Vera tugged her scarf off and lay it on the seat beside her. "Grandma has a sharp eye, and if Snowball came down this way at all, Grandma will know."

Libby hesitated. She wanted to find out about Snowball, but she hadn't met Grandma Feuder yet. Grandma wasn't a true relative, but everyone called her Grandma. "I don't know her and she doesn't know me."

Vera patted Libby's cold hand. "Would you feel better if I went?"

"Yes!" Libby hated meeting new people. They always asked how she liked living with the Johnsons and how it felt to be a "welfare kid." Some of them were polite enough to say "foster child." Libby didn't want to talk about being a welfare kid and living with the Johnsons. She didn't want to talk about Toby Smart or the fact that he would soon be adopted and become a real member of the Johnson family.

Vera got out of the car and walked up to the house. Libby squirmed in the seat, then quickly opened the car door and jumped out. She would meet Grandma Feuder, and she would not feel bad that she wasn't a real Johnson, nor ever likely to become one.

A dog barked and ran to sniff Libby. She patted his head and talked softly to him. She walked around a mud puddle onto the wet grass. A movement beside an old barn caught her attention. She stopped, her head up and her eyes wide. A tall boy with light brown hair, dressed in a fleece-lined jacket, stood peering around the side of the barn. He jumped back out of sight when he saw Libby. She frowned. Who was the boy? Grandma lived alone. Was he here to steal something? Could he have stolen Snowball?

Libby dashed across the wet yard, the dog at her heels. "I want to talk to you," she shouted. "Don't run away!"

The sandy-haired boy stepped out and

stood with his arms folded in a hostile stance. His jeans and jacket looked new. "Yeah, what do you want?"

Libby stopped in front of him. He stood a head taller than she did and was just as thin. "My horse is missing. She's all white and almost a year old. Have you seen her?"

"No." He turned away.

"Wait!" Libby wanted to jerk him around and make him talk to her. "Are you sure? You might have seen her since you weren't in school today. At least you didn't ride our bus."

"I told you I didn't see a horse." He looked bored and impatient.

"I gotta find Snowball! I'd just die if she got hit by a car."

"You should take better care of her." He picked up a stick and broke it with a snap. He tossed a piece of it and the dog raced after it, barking happily. "You got other horses. What do you need with this one?"

Libby took a deep breath before she burst with anger. "Snowball is mine. The Johnsons gave her to me for my twelfth birthday."

The boy frowned. "You talk like they aren't your family."

Libby's face flamed as she looked away. "They are now."

"You're adopted?"

Libby glared at him. "That's none of your business!"

"I see. You're a poor relative that they were forced to take in."

"I am not!" Libby's hazel eyes glittered angrily. "I'm a foster child, but now I belong to the Johnson family. They want me! Chuck and Vera are my parents now."

"Hey, you don't have to get mad," he said, surprised by her fiery response. "What's your name? I'm Adam Feuder."

"Is Grandma Feuder your real grandma?"

"She's my great-grandma." The boy stuffed his hands deep into his pockets and hunched deeper into his coat. "I'm 13 years old. Who's the oldest Johnson boy?"

"Ben's the oldest. He's 13, like you. Susan is almost 12. I'm 12 and Kevin is 10 and Toby is 9. Toby's the redheaded little boy and Kevin's the blond." Libby looked down at the tips of her muddy boots. "I'm Libby."

"I watched you all get on the bus this morning and get off this afternoon."

Libby frowned. Adam sounded as if he resented their going to school. "Why don't you go to school?"

He shrugged. "I take correspondence

classes. Sometimes I'm home-schooled. I'm never in one place long enough to go to a regular school. I probably won't be here for long."

"I sure wish you had seen Snowball." Libby's shoulders drooped as she turned toward the house. "Maybe your grandma saw her."

Adam followed Libby to the front porch, where Vera and Grandma Feuder were talking. Two dogs crowded around Grandma's legs.

Vera slid her arm around Libby. "Libby, I want you to meet Grandma Feuder. I see you've already met Adam."

Libby managed a smile as Grandma firmly shook hands with her, telling her how glad she was to finally meet the girl whom the Johnsons had prayed into their home.

"I'm sorry about Snowball. I believe Jesus will show you where she is." Grandma's wrinkled face glowed happily. "There's nothing that he doesn't know, and he loves doing good things for you."

Adam made a sharp sound, then abruptly walked away.

"Adam doesn't believe in a personal relationship with God," said Grandma, watching him walk away. She turned a smiling face again to Libby. "You pray for him, OK?"

"I will." Libby suddenly felt warm all over as she remembered how she'd asked Jesus to be her personal Savior just a short time ago.

Grandma patted Libby's hand. "Snowball will be found, Libby. God will answer you."

Vera kissed Grandma's cheek. "I haven't seen any of your prayers go unanswered yet. It would be wonderful to have your faith."

"You have it, Vera. Even Libby does. God's Word says that he gives each of us a measure of faith. We have to learn to put it to use, that's all. Put it to use and it'll grow."

Libby thought about that, then nodded. It made sense. God had answered her prayers before. He would answer her prayer to find Snowball.

"Come see me again, Libby," said Grandma, tugging her coat closer around her thin body. "I'd like to get to know you, and I'd like you and Adam to get acquainted."

"I'd be happy to come back." Libby was surprised at her words, and even more surprised when she realized she meant them.

Grandma
Feuder

SLOWLY Libby climbed out of the school
bus and headed toward the house. She didn't
want to go to the barn and be disappointed if
Snowball was still missing. Her hopes had
been dashed once already when Snowball
wasn't found the night before.

"Hurry up, Libby," said Susan, impatiently
tugging Libby's arm toward the barn. "Snowball is probably in her stall right now. How
will you find out if you don't look?"

A sharp wind blew against Libby, making
her shiver. It would be terrible to look in the
barn and find out that Snowball was still
gone.

"I'll look for you," said Kevin, punching his

glasses against his face, his blue eyes round. "Toby and I will look."

Toby flipped his hood over his red hair and raced after Kevin.

Libby blinked hard to keep from crying. She would not cry in front of Ben and Susan.

Ben pushed his red hair off his forehead, and it flopped back down as he shook his head. "The fence wasn't down. I don't know how Snowball got out. Don't feel bad, Elizabeth."

Libby blinked in surprise. Usually only Dad called her Elizabeth. It sounded nice coming from Ben. Libby took a deep breath. "I'll try not to, Ben."

"We prayed about it; now we'll just wait and trust," said Ben as they walked slowly up the wide driveway.

Goosy Poosy honked and ran toward them with his white wings spread and his long neck out. Libby's heart skipped a beat and she stepped closer to Susan.

"Hi, Goosy Poosy," said Susan, holding her arms out to the big white goose. "I'm so glad to see you!" The goose rubbed his long neck up and down Susan's arm. "Did you miss me today? Are you hungry?"

Libby wrinkled her nose. How could Susan

allow that goose to rub against her? What if
Goosy Poosy got mad and pecked Susan?

A big black-and-tan collie raced around the
house and ran right to Libby. She hugged
him, pressing her face against his neck. "I
love you, Rex," she whispered so that Ben
and Susan couldn't hear her.

Ben looked up at the gray sky. "It looks
like it's going to rain again. We'd better hurry
and get the chores done. Race you, girls." His
long legs flying, he dashed up the driveway.

Libby laughed as she raced after him. She
could run almost as fast as Ben. Rex barked at
her heels. She heard Susan close behind her
while Goosy Poosy honked wildly.

Just as Libby hung up her jacket beside
Dad's red-plaid farm coat, Kevin and Toby
burst through the door.

"She's not there," said Kevin, panting hard.

"Snowball's still missing," said Toby, his
eyes wide, "unless Mom knows where she is."

Libby leaned weakly against her jacket, her
face hidden from the others. Would they ever
find Snowball?

"Hi, kids." Vera stood in the doorway, smiling a cheerful welcome. "We have bananas
and milk for a snack." She tugged her blue
sweater down over her denim skirt and

walked over to Libby. She slid her arms around her. "Snowball will turn up, honey. Don't worry. This is the time to trust God for the answer. We won't give up looking, but we won't become anxious either."

Libby managed a smile, then walked with the others to the large kitchen. She was able to enjoy a banana and a glass of cold milk. She looked up when Vera set a grocery bag beside her.

"Libby, please take this to Grandma Feuder. I baked some cookies and put in a half gallon of milk and some other goodies for her and Adam." Vera turned to the others around the table. "Kevin and Susan, you split Libby's chores between you." Vera laughed. "You know Grandma. She won't allow anyone to leave without a nice, long chat."

Libby bit her lower lip. What would Grandma find to chat about with her? She looked helplessly at Susan. "I'll do your chores if you'll go."

Susan laughed and shook her head. Her red-gold hair bounced around her slender shoulders. "Not me. I like Grandma, but I have too much homework to do tonight. Besides, you'll like hearing all her stories. She'll probably give you a dozen cookies to eat while you listen to her."

Vera kissed Libby's cheek. "You'll enjoy listening to Grandma. Be back by supper, sooner if you can leave without hurting Grandma's feelings."

"See if Adam will come down to play ball sometime," said Ben, pushing back his chair and standing up. "Or maybe he'd like to go riding with us when we take the horses out."

"I'll ask him," said Libby hesitantly. From the little she'd seen of Adam, she thought she already knew his answer. Adam wouldn't be interested.

Ten minutes later Libby knocked on Grandma Feuder's door. The dogs inside the house barked loudly. Then Libby heard Grandma commanding them to hush. Grandma opened the door wide and smiled as Libby entered. "Now, I'm going to call you Elizabeth if you don't mind. Elizabeth is a beautiful name for a lovely young girl."

Libby blushed. Maybe Grandma would think her face was red from being in the hot room. Nobody else thought she was lovely. The thought made her feel very good. She smiled and held the bag out to Grandma. "Mom asked me to give this to you." As Grandma unpacked the groceries, Libby

13

looked around for Adam. Was he out sneaking around the barn again?

"Have a chair, Elizabeth." Grandma tapped the cane seat of a banister-back chair. "Sit right here, next to Teddy."

Libby giggled as she looked at the worn brown-and-tan bear on the chair next to her. He had big brown eyes made of buttons. Part of the fur had worn off his face and stomach. "Does Teddy always eat with you?"

"Always." Grandma patted the bear's head. "This is his chair, and he stays put unless I move him so that someone can have his chair."

"Kids that visit you must have a lot of fun playing with him."

"Oh my, no! He's not a toy. Nobody has permission to play with him. Adam always wants to pick him up and punch him around. I don't allow that at all." Grandma set a glass of milk in front of Libby. "I want you to enjoy a few cookies with me, too. I'll save some for Adam."

Grandma sat down with a mug of hot tea. She took a sip, then set the cup on the table. "Adam went for a long walk. He's a strange boy, Elizabeth. I know he's very lonely some-times; then at other times he acts as if he

hates everyone around him." She sipped her
tea again, then set down the cup and wrapped
her wrinkled fingers around it. She was
dressed in a flowered cotton dress that
buttoned to just below the waist. Her white
hair was combed neatly.

Libby noticed that Grandma's faded blue
eyes sparkled one minute and were thoughtful the next. Just a few months ago she
wouldn't have been sensitive to the feelings
of anyone but herself. But now she sensed
that something was bothering Grandma.
Grandma chatted away about her life on the
farm, but Libby knew her mind wasn't always
on what she was saying. Libby wondered why
Adam was living with his great-grandmother,
but she didn't want to pry.

Finally Libby dabbed her mouth with a yellow
napkin, stood up, and said, "I'd better go home
now. Thank you for the cookies and milk."

"Thank you for coming, Elizabeth."
Grandma stood up too, and immediately the
two dogs were at her side. "Thank Vera for
the things she sent. I appreciate them."
Grandma sighed. "I have a lot on my mind
today, Elizabeth, and I guess I'm not very
good company."

"I liked visiting you," she said. And to her

surprise, she meant it. "I'm sorry that you're upset over something."

"I got a letter today from my son-in-law, and he's up to his old tricks." Grandma chuckled. "I won't bore you with all that, but come back again soon, Elizabeth. I'm sorry you haven't found Snowball yet, but she'll be found. God will answer."

Libby wanted to hug Grandma. She sounded so sure of herself, and so sure of God.

"You pray for me, Elizabeth. Pray that my son-in-law won't be able to put anything over on me. He sure is going to try. And if I know him at all, he'll keep on trying."

Libby frowned. How dare anyone try to hurt Grandma! And why would anyone want to? "I *will* pray, Grandma."

"Thank you, honey." She hugged Libby, then walked to the door with her, the dogs close behind. "Come back again soon. Maybe get acquainted with Adam. He needs friends his own age."

"Tell him to come play ball or go horseback riding with us."

The wind almost took Libby's breath away as she walked down the driveway. She caught a glimpse of Adam and decided to invite him over herself. Her steps were muffled as she walked across the grass toward him. His back was turned and his shoulders shook. His face was pressed into his arms as he leaned against a wooden fence. Libby could hear his wild sobbing. She hesitated, then turned quietly and walked away. He would be very embarrassed if he knew she had seen and heard him crying.

Slowly Libby walked home. Why was Adam crying? Maybe she should have said something to him, tried to help him. She felt like crying too. Did Grandma know that Adam was unhappy? Did anybody know? Suddenly Libby stopped. God knew. God knew Adam's thoughts and feelings. She would pray for him. That was the very best thing she could do for Adam now.

Adam

BEN impatiently flung his red windbreaker over his shoulder. He kicked a clump of dirt along the side of the road, sending it crumbling over the pavement. "I don't know why we should get acquainted with Adam Feuder. He doesn't want to see us. You know how he acted two days ago when we were there asking about Snowball again."

Susan ran a few steps to catch up to Libby and Ben. "If Libby thinks we should get to know Adam, then I think we should try. I can't understand why you're acting so crabby about it, Ben."

"I'm not crabby! I just don't like Adam Feuder. He thinks he's so big!" Ben frowned at Libby. "I don't see why you want us to get acquainted."

"He must be really lonely," said Libby.

She hadn't told them about seeing Adam sobbing last week when she'd taken the groceries to Grandma. But she hadn't forgotten. She wanted to do something to make him happy. Adam never seemed in the mood to get acquainted. Maybe if Ben and Susan went with her, Adam would be more friendly. At times she felt more upset over Adam than over not finding Snowball.

A small black-and-white dog ran out of the Feuders' driveway and barked excitedly, sniffing first at Ben, then at Susan, then at Libby. Libby patted his head. "Hush, Lapdog," said Libby firmly. She giggled. Grandma had told her that she had named him Lapdog because every time she sat on the porch, the dog jumped on her lap to be held.

Lapdog stopped barking and whimpered a welcome, his small body twisting and turning with each wag of his short, stubby tail.

Adam stood on the porch, leaning against a pillar, his hands in his jeans pockets. The brown sweater he wore made his light brown eyes appear darker. He didn't smile or move. "Grandma's not home. She won't be home until dinnertime."

"We know," said Ben. "We came over to see you."

Libby stopped on the porch step and stared at Grandma's teddy bear flopped on its side on the porch swing. "Adam! Why is this bear out here?" She watched the color creep up his neck into his face.

"I can bring that bear out anytime I want." Adam picked it up by the ear and held it high. "Want to see it fly?"

Libby lunged for the bear, grabbing it firmly. "Grandma doesn't allow anyone to touch Teddy and you know it! Let me take him back to his chair."

Abruptly Adam released the bear. "Who wants to fight over a silly bear? Put it away before I toss it to the dogs."

Libby heard Susan asking Adam about his family as she carried Teddy into the kitchen. Carefully she set him on his chair, then hurried out of the house into the bright sunlight. Adam was answering Susan's questions as curtly and rudely as possible. Ben was petting Lapdog and trying to pretend he wasn't getting angry at Adam's answers. Libby caught Ben's eye and smiled. He frowned.

Adam glared at Libby. "Do you still think I know where your white horse is?"

"Of course not," said Libby. "We know the

police are looking for Snowball. We've looked everywhere that we know to look." Libby could tell that Susan and Ben were getting very impatient with Adam. "We came to visit you so you wouldn't be lonely."

"Who says I'm lonely?" Adam turned and walked toward the chicken house. The yard was almost dry. The wind would soon dry the grass completely.

Susan ran after Adam, her ponytail bobbing merrily. "We want to be friends."

Adam stopped and frowned angrily. "Who wants to be friends with you?"

"Let's go home," said Ben gruffly.

Libby caught Ben's arm. "No, wait." She looked imploringly at Adam. "We really do want to be friends."

Ben tugged free. "We could play ball."

"Who wants to?" Adam picked up a black walnut and pitched it at a red hen scratching in the dirt inside the chicken pen. The walnut almost hit the hen and she ran across the pen, squawking with her wings flapping. "We could see who could hit the most chickens with these walnuts," said Adam, bending to pick up another walnut.

Libby leaped toward Adam, her fists flying. "Don't you dare hurt those chickens!"

Adam stopped her and held her back so she couldn't hit him. Then he laughed. "I give up. I'll leave the chickens alone. I can't promise we'll be friends, but I won't send you home."

Susan tugged on Libby's arm. "He said he'd quit, Libby. Let's think of something to do."

Libby stepped back, breathing hard. She felt like punching Adam for laughing at her. Finally she laughed too. She turned to Ben, then stopped laughing when she saw the scowl on his face. Why was Ben acting so strangely? Usually he made friends easily. For some reason he didn't like Adam. Libby sighed and turned away.

"I know what we can do!" exclaimed Susan, her blue eyes sparkling. "We can go to our house and go horseback riding. Can you ride, Adam?"

He shrugged, but Libby had a feeling he was excited. "I've only ridden English style, but I'm sure I can try Western if that's all you have."

"We like what we have," snapped Ben. He walked down the driveway, then turned impatiently. "Are you coming or not?"

"Might as well," said Adam. "You two can go on ahead. I'll walk with Libby."

Libby flushed.

"We'll all walk together," said Ben with a scowl.

Susan giggled and nudged Libby. Libby wanted to die right on the spot. She was glad that Adam wasn't looking at her right then.

They walked in silence for a few feet. Suddenly Adam stopped and pointed at two people riding toward them on bikes. "Who is that girl?" he asked sharply.

"Brenda Wilkens," answered Susan. "And that's her brother Joe with her. They live in that big white house just past ours."

"I don't like her," said Adam. "She always rides past and says hi to me."

Libby hid a grin. Brenda would really be angry if she heard a good-looking boy say that he didn't like her. She thought all the boys liked her all the time.

"This should be good," whispered Susan as Brenda and Joe stopped beside Ben and Adam.

Libby tried not to laugh, but she couldn't help herself. She ducked her head when Brenda glared at her.

"Hi," said Joe, smiling. When he smiled, even his dark brown eyes smiled.

"I'm Brenda Wilkens," said Brenda, looking right at Adam. "I've seen you at the Feuder place."

"He lives there," said Susan.

"Grandma Feuder is his great-grandma," said Libby.

Brenda lifted her chin and stared at Libby, then looked away. "Ben, would you and Adam like to go bike riding with us?" She flipped her long dark hair over her slender shoulders. "It's such a beautiful day."

Libby remembered the time in church when she'd pinched Brenda on the back of the leg. Suddenly she wanted to do it again, only harder. She knew she should be ashamed of herself for thinking that way. She looked right at Brenda. "We're going horseback riding."

"Go ahead, then," snapped Brenda. "I didn't ask you anyway, welfare kid." She smiled sweetly at Adam. "I'm surprised your parents allow you to talk to this girl. She's a welfare kid, you know."

Libby clenched her fists. Her heart raced and she wanted to sink through the ground.

"I already know that Elizabeth is a foster child," said Adam. "But she's my friend. I like her. You're the girl my parents wouldn't want me to talk to!"

Brenda flushed and backed away.

Libby gasped as she lifted shining eyes to Adam. He smiled at her and she smiled widely.

"Let's get out of here, Joe," said Brenda. "I'm going to be sick." She jumped on her bike and rode away, her black hair flying out behind her.

"Now you've asked for it," Joe said to Adam, grinning. "My sister will get even with you for saying that to her. I'll try to warn you in advance when she's plotting something." Joe rode after his sister, bending low over his bike, his shirt puffing with air.

No one spoke for a long time. A car whizzed past. Finally Susan said, "I think I'm going to like you after all, Adam."

Adam shrugged. "I know a lot of kids like Brenda Wilkens. I know how to handle them." He shook his head and frowned. "It's you three I can't understand. You're different. You're going to take some getting used to."

Slowly they resumed walking along the road. Libby tried to think of the words to say that would explain to Adam what made them different. It was easy enough in her own mind to say that Christ made them different, but saying it out loud was too difficult. Maybe when she and Adam were alone some time she could tell him how she used to be and how Jesus had changed her.

As they turned into the Johnsons' driveway, Adam walked close beside Libby. "I really am sorry about Snowball being gone," he said. "I did try to find her for you, but I didn't see her anywhere."

"Thank you for trying." Libby kept her eyes on the gravel driveway. "And thanks for saying that to Brenda, and for calling me Elizabeth."

"That's OK. I guess I do want to be friends."

"Me too," she said softly.

Rex ran to her side, barking. She was glad for the interruption. She patted him, then introduced him to Adam.

Goosy Poosy honked noisily and ran toward them. Susan stopped him, then knelt down, her arms around him as she looked up at Adam. "This is our pet goose. Goosy Poosy, meet Libby's new friend, Adam Feuder."

Libby frowned at Susan's teasing. Adam didn't seem to mind as he knelt beside Susan and stroked the goose.

"Aren't we going riding today?" asked Ben, stuffing his hands deep into his pockets.

"Sure we are," said Libby, wondering why

Ben was acting so impatient. Ben was usually the nicest person around. Something was wrong—but what? She ran toward the horse barn with the others. Maybe she would have a chance later to talk to him alone. She had noticed the difference in Ben ever since Adam came to town. But that didn't make a difference to Ben, did it?

The Teddy Bear Mystery

GRANDMA Feuder shook her finger angrily at Adam while Libby cringed in a chair beside the kitchen table. "Adam, you tell me this minute what you did with Teddy. I've told you over and over not to touch that bear!" Tears sparkled in Grandma's faded blue eyes. She wiped them away with the corner of her flowered apron. "Oh, Adam! Where is Teddy?"

Adam was gripping the back of the kitchen chair in front of him. "Why would I have taken that silly bear? I don't want it. I'm too old to play with bears."

Libby could tell by Adam's face that he knew exactly where the bear was. She bit her lower lip to keep from saying something to him.

Grandma sank down in a chair and pushed a loose tendril of wavy white hair off her face.

"Adam, that bear is very important to me. Please, bring the bear in here and put him on that chair again."

"Why is that old bear so important?" asked Adam gruffly.

"My grandson Bob gave me that bear when he was 12 years old. I told him someday I would give it back to him." Grandma frowned sternly. "Now get Teddy and put him on his chair."

"How do you know I took him? Maybe Libby did."

Libby blinked in surprise. "I did not! Adam, you know I didn't."

Grandma sighed unhappily. "Don't tease me, Adam. I'm tired and it's hot and I can't take it today."

Libby could hear the tree toads and bull-frogs through the open door. It was hard to remember the long cold winter now that it was spring. And it was terrible to hear cross words on such a beautiful evening. She frowned at Adam. She wanted to shout at him to get the bear and bring it back. She clenched her fists and glared at Adam.

Finally Adam turned away. "The bear is in my closet. I'll get it." He stomped out of the room. The small black dog followed him.

Grandma shook her head with a loud sigh.

"I don't know what comes over that boy. One day he's as good as can be. The next, he's up to all kinds of naughty tricks. He's not happy, Elizabeth. I thought it would help for you children to make friends with him. He seems to like you well enough, but the others—well, you know how he is with them."

"I know. While we were riding today he teased Susan until she ran into the house crying. Ben got mad at him, and Ben doesn't get mad often. They don't want to try getting acquainted again."

"Why do you have patience with the boy, Elizabeth?" Grandma eyed Libby thoughtfully.

Libby laughed. Should she tell Grandma about seeing Adam sobbing hard that day? No, she'd better not. "I guess Adam isn't scared of me like he is of the others." She laughed again. "Why would anyone be scared of a skinny girl like me? I couldn't hurt him if I tried."

Grandma chuckled, then sobered instantly. She pressed her hands to her heart. "There are a lot of ways to hurt people, Elizabeth girl. Hurting them physically is just one small way."

Libby shivered. She didn't know exactly

what Grandma meant, but she knew Grandma was hurt in a way she wouldn't talk about. Tears pricked Libby's eyes.

Adam walked in and plopped the bear on its chair. "Here's your stuffed bear. I don't know what's so important about that old thing."

Grandma picked him up and looked him over carefully. "Are you all right, Teddy? Are you hurt?"

Libby frowned. Why *was* the bear so important? Grandma was acting funny. Dad said some old people got strange as they grew older. But Grandma didn't seem old most of the time.

"I guess you didn't hurt him," said Grandma in relief as she lovingly set Teddy on his chair again. "Sit down, Adam, and have a cup of cocoa and a warm cinnamon roll with Elizabeth. You could use some meat on those bones. You and Elizabeth could pass for drinking straws, skinny ones at that." She chuckled as she patted Adam's arm.

Adam jerked away and pushed open the screen door. "I'm not hungry. I'm going for a walk."

"Don't stay after dark. I don't want you getting lost." Grandma stuffed two rolls in a plastic bag. "Here, Adam, take these with you and eat 'em as you walk. Or feed a bird or squirrel." She smiled at Adam, then kissed his cheek. "Thank you for returning my bear, Adam. I love you."

Libby could tell that the kiss pleased Adam, but that he was embarrassed and didn't want her or Grandma to know it. He grabbed the bag and rushed out, slamming the screen door behind him. "Have a good walk," Grandma said. Adam called to the dog and walked away, whistling out of tune.

Libby's heart swelled as she observed the love on Grandma's face. "You'll miss Adam if he ever leaves here, won't you, Grandma?"

"I sure will. He's a lot like his granddaddy was—my son. Larkin was tall and lean like Adam. And he had his quiet times and his naughty times like Adam. Sometimes I think I'm young again and it's my boy teasing the dogs and whistling out of tune. Then I remember he's my great-grandson and I'm an old woman alone." Grandma patted the black dog on the head. "But I'm not alone, Elizabeth. I have Jesus." Grandma smiled at Libby. "And I have my dogs and my friends, too."

Libby wondered what her own real grandma was like. She'd never seen either of her parents' mothers. "How many grandchildren and great-grandchildren do you have, Grandma?"

Grandma wrinkled her forehead and tipped her head in thought. "My son Larkin had four children—Lucy, Christina, Molly, and Jim. The girls have three children each, or maybe Molly has four now. They live in Montana and I never see them anymore." Grandma took a sip of tea. "My grandson, Jim, has only one son, Adam. Jim and his wife, Shirley, travel a lot and I don't see much of them. They left Adam with Larkin for a while, but he just isn't up to having a boy around, so I took him for now. Larkin isn't feeling as well as he should be." Grandma picked up Teddy and hugged him close.

"Do you have any daughters, Grandma?" Libby asked, taking a cookie from the plate on the table.

"Yes. My daughter Jane married Steve Dupont. They had a son named Bob, and when he was only 12, Steve died. That's when Bob bought Teddy for me." Grandma dabbed tears from her eyes with the corner of her apron. She cleared her throat. "Two years later, Jane married a man named Henry Comstock. He's caused trouble ever since. Bob ran away from home a couple times when he was 16. After the second time, Jane was so angry that she told her son she didn't want to see him again—and she never did. Bob's 25 now, and Jane died last fall. I saw him at the funeral. I told him I still had Teddy and that I wanted to give him back. But with Henry, his stepdad, interfering in my life, I don't know if I'll ever have that chance." Grandma stopped, then laughed. "What am I talking on and on for, Elizabeth? All of this is in God's hands." Grandma patted Libby's knee. "Let's talk about you for a while, Elizabeth girl."

Libby licked her suddenly dry lips. "There's nothing to say." She didn't want to talk about her real mother—how she had neglected Libby—or how the court had placed Libby in one foster home after another until the Johnson family had taken her. Talking about her father wouldn't hurt quite so much, even though he had deserted her when she was three. He'd sent her a secret puzzle box for her twelfth birthday. That's when she learned that he loved her, and she'd learned to love him. Then all the hurt and bitterness she'd had toward him vanished. But she preferred living on the farm with the Johnsons. "I'm happy living with the Johnson family," she said. "They're my family now and I love them."

"And they love you."

Libby smiled dreamily. "I know." Having

someone love her was wonderful. She had been 11 years old before anyone had truly loved her. Even now it seemed too good to be true. "I'm glad I live with the Johnson family." Libby looked at Grandma and realized she wasn't listening.

Grandma stared at Teddy and stroked his worn fur. "Bob said he'd be back to get this bear in April." Her eyes misted with tears. She looked up at Libby. "Elizabeth, I need to ask a big favor of you. Will you do something for me?"

"Of course I will, Grandma." Libby jumped up and stood close beside Grandma's chair. "I'll do anything for you. Honest." Libby's hazel eyes sparkled with excitement. She folded her hands to keep Grandma from seeing them tremble. She knew Grandma was going to ask her to do something very special.

"I can't explain my reason for asking you, but it's important." Grandma pressed Teddy into Libby's arms. Libby frowned. "Elizabeth, I want you to take Teddy home to your room and keep him there. Don't give him to anyone but Bob Dupont, my grandson. I'll write him a letter and tell him about you and where you live. I'll tell him he can get Teddy from you in case anything happens to me."

Libby shivered. What could happen to

Grandma? She tightened her hold on Teddy. "Won't you miss your bear, Grandma?"

Grandma pushed back her chair and stood up. She smoothed down her apron and tried to smile. "I have Adam now. And I think Teddy will be safer at your house."

Safer? Libby swallowed hard. What did Grandma mean?

Grandma clutched Libby's arms. "Promise to keep him in your room and don't ever, ever give him to anyone but Bob. Promise me that, Elizabeth."

It was hard to talk around the big lump in her throat. Libby's voice came out squeaky. "I promise, Grandma."

"I know you'll take good care of him." Grandma kissed Libby's flushed cheek. "If I can, I'll tell you the whole story someday."

"I'd . . . I'd better go home now." Libby walked slowly to the door, hugging the bear to her chest. The dogs stayed close beside Grandma. Libby stopped at the door and looked back. Tears were sliding down Grandma's wrinkled cheeks. Libby felt like crying too.

The
Hidden Barn

LIBBY slipped behind a large oak tree, then sped down a well-worn path through the woods. It was hard to act cheerful while playing hide-and-seek with the others today. She was still feeling terrible because they hadn't yet found Snowball.

Mom and Dad had thought it strange when Grandma sent Teddy home with Libby. But if it made Grandma feel better, they'd said Libby should keep Teddy. Susan was convinced a mystery was involved, and she wanted to solve it. Ben had asked if Grandma was just trying to keep the bear out of Adam's way.

Libby sighed as she stopped for breath. The sun shone brightly through the still bare trees. It was April, but spring was late this year. Would Bob Dupont come soon for Teddy? Teddy looked right at home on her bed beside her stuffed dog, Pinky.

Last night during family devotions, Dad had prayed for Grandma Feuder and Bob Dupont. Libby had felt a little better.

Adam was "it" for hide-and-seek. He would never think to look for her so far away from base. Libby managed a smile. Would Adam give up and allow her to run home free? She had seen Ben hide behind Grandma's chicken coop. Susan had been running toward a large maple just behind the house. Maybe if Adam acted right, Ben and Susan would start liking him. Libby shook her head. Sometimes it was hard even for her to like him. He had been angry when Grandma told him that she'd sent Teddy home with Libby. Teddy was causing too much trouble.

Libby slipped behind another tree and ran on until she reached a clearing. She pushed her hair back and lifted her face to a gentle breeze. She gasped in surprise when she saw a weathered gray barn in the middle of the clearing. The fence around the barn looked as if it had come from an old-time picture. Some of the poles were split and others round. Was she still on Feuder property?

Slowly she walked toward the small barn. A noise inside made her stop in her tracks. She pressed her hand over her mouth to keep from crying out. Maybe someone was staying in the barn. Or maybe it was only an animal she heard inside. Grandma had said that Henry Comstock was causing trouble for her. He might be in the barn just waiting to make more trouble.

Just before the game of hide-and-seek, Libby and Susan had been sitting on the porch with Grandma Feuder. "Henry Comstock will do anything to get me away from here," Grandma had said as she rubbed her hand over Lapdog. "He's my son-in-law. He married my daughter Jane about two years after her first husband died." Grandma often repeated things when she talked to Libby. But she hadn't said how or why Henry Comstock would try to force Grandma away from her farm.

Libby stood beside the old gray barn, shivers running up and down her spine. What would she do if Henry Comstock was inside the barn? How would she know him if she saw him? She shook her head impatiently. She was being foolish. Henry Comstock was probably far away in his own home or at work, or maybe he was off visiting whatever other family he had.

A nicker inside the barn made Libby's pulse quicken. There was a horse inside! She opened the door with a loud creak, then stared in surprise. Snowball was tied in the first open stall. She nickered a glad welcome and turned her head as far as the rope would allow.

"Snowball!" Libby rushed to her and flung her arms around her neck. "Snowball! Oh, Snowball!" Tears streamed down Libby's cheeks as she stood back and looked again to make sure she wasn't dreaming.

Slowly Libby ran her hands down Snowball's chest and legs. "You're real! You aren't hurt!" Libby saw the feed that Snowball had been eating, then spotted a bucket of water on the floor.

Libby's hazel eyes sparked with anger. Who had tied Snowball in the barn? Who had kept her here secretly all this time? This had to be Grandma Feuder's barn. Adam must have done it. Adam!

Libby clenched her fists. "Wait until I get my hands on you, Adam Feuder! You'll be sorry!" She untied the rope and led Snowball from the barn and through the woods. As she got closer to Grandma's house, she heard the shouts and laughter from the others.

Toby saw her first. He ran toward her, shouting excitedly. "Oh, Libby, you found her! Where was she?"

Libby walked on until she stood in front of Adam. She doubled her fist and pulled it back to sock him. Then she stopped. She couldn't hit him. She tried to yell at him, but her voice was gone. She saw his frown and knew he could see her anger.

"What's the matter?" he asked softly. "Where was Snowball?"

Libby opened her mouth, but nothing came out. Slowly she lowered her hand and shook her head.

Grandma hurried from the house, her face glowing happily. "I knew God would answer, Elizabeth. I knew you'd find Snowball."

"Where was she?" asked Ben, rubbing his hands up and down Snowball's white back, legs, and shoulders.

"Ask Adam," cried Libby. "Ask Adam about the hidden barn back in the woods!"

"Me?" Adam's eyes widened in alarm. "Why ask me?"

"What do you mean, Libby?" asked Susan, dancing around in excitement.

"What barn?" asked Kevin.

"You don't mean that small barn back in

the trees!" cried Grandma, wrapping her hands in her apron. "How did she get in there?"

"Adam put her there. He tied her in the first stall, and he's been feeding and watering her." Libby's voice cracked and she couldn't say anything more. She watched as Ben walked slowly toward Adam. Adam backed away, almost tripping over Lapdog.

"I didn't know about the barn," he said gruffly. "Why should I tie up that horse and keep her from Elizabeth? I wouldn't do that."

"Then who did?" asked Ben, his fists doubled at his sides.

"It wasn't me!" cried Adam. He turned to Grandma. "Tell them I didn't do it. If it had been a joke, I'd have admitted it. But I didn't know about the barn, and I didn't know Snowball was there."

Grandma patted Adam's arm. "I believe you." She looked at Ben, then at Libby. "Adam didn't do it. I know him. But who *would* do such a terrible thing? Everyone knows how upset Elizabeth has been over Snowball. I think we should call Chuck and tell him about this."

"I know who would do such a thing," said Kevin, pushing his glasses up on his nose.

The sun made his blond hair look even lighter.

"Who?" asked Toby, tugging his shirt down over his jeans.

"Brenda Wilkens," said Kevin in a hushed voice as he looked at the others.

"I'll get her for this," said Adam angrily.

Ben stood with his fists on his hips, his feet apart. "We don't know if it was Brenda. Kevin's only guessing."

"Oh, you don't like to think Brenda does anything bad," said Susan, flipping her long red-gold ponytail over her shoulder. "You always stick up for her even when she's mean to Libby."

Libby took a deep breath as she stared intently at Adam. "Did you take Snowball, Adam?"

He shook his head. "No, Elizabeth, I really didn't."

Libby ran her hand lovingly along Snowball's neck. "I would really like to know if Brenda Wilkens did it. She hates me. She could have done it."

"And she could've tied him in that barn so you would think Adam did it," said Susan. "I say Brenda did it."

"Kids, don't jump to conclusions," said

Grandma. "You don't want to hurt her by accusing her of something that she might not have done."

"Hey, this is the time of day Brenda and Joe ride their bikes," said Susan. "Let's walk Snowball home and see what Brenda says about it."

"I'm going with you," said Adam, walking over to stand beside Libby. "I want to know the truth." He lowered his voice so only Libby could hear. "I'm glad you found Snowball."

"Thanks." Libby wanted to tell him how glad she was that he hadn't taken Snowball, but the words wouldn't come. She smiled, then looked quickly away.

"Come on, Libby," said Kevin impatiently. "Brenda and Joe will be coming this way soon."

Libby led Snowball down the driveway and to the side of the road. The *click, click* of hooves on pavement was loud in the stillness. A car sped past, and Libby held tighter to the rope as Snowball pranced and pulled away from the sound.

"Here they come," whispered Toby.

"Don't be mean," said Ben with a scowl.

"I'd like to punch her hard," said Kevin.

Libby giggled nervously. "Don't worry,

boys. I'll take care of everything." She knew Ben was remembering the time she had punched Brenda in the nose and made it bleed.

"I'll do the talking," said Ben. "I'm the oldest and I'll handle this."

"You'll be too nice," said Susan.

"It's my horse and I'll handle it," said Libby, her pointed chin high in the air.

"But you'd better not punch her," said Susan. "Mom and Dad would get mad."

Libby's heart beat faster as Brenda and Joe reached them. Libby prayed quickly for help in discovering the truth. She felt her anger leave and actually smiled as Brenda stood astride her bike. Libby watched as Brenda's face went pale, then flushed red.

"Thanks for taking such good care of Snowball," said Libby, smiling at Brenda cheerfully. "I didn't like it that she was gone all that time, but I am glad you took good care of her."

Brenda gasped.

Joe glared at his sister. "You're mean, Brenda. Wait until I tell Mom on you. Can't you ever stay out of trouble?"

"Shut up!" cried Brenda, glaring at Joe. "Mind your own business."

Libby knew the others were waiting to see

how she would handle the situation. "You don't have to tell on her, Joe," said Libby, sliding her arm over Snowball's neck. "I'm glad to have Snowball back. I know I found her because we all prayed. Jesus answered our prayer. And Brenda, I'm glad you didn't let her starve. You did a good job."

Brenda's mouth was open, her face fiery red. She flipped back her dark hair, pushed off on the bike pedal, and raced toward home.

Susan giggled. "I think that's what Mom calls heaping coals of fire on her head."

"I'm sorry about this," said Joe, watching his sister disappear down the road. "I don't know why she's so mean."

"I think it's because she isn't a Christian," said Toby. "She doesn't know how to be good. We have Jesus to help us."

"Oh, brother," said Adam. He turned and stalked away.

Joe was quiet a long time. "I think I'd like to be a Christian too."

"I'm glad," said Ben. "Dad says you can pray to receive Jesus anywhere." He paused. "Joe, we can pray right here if you want."

"I'd like that," said Joe firmly.

Tears filled Libby's eyes as Ben and Joe prayed, asking Jesus to wash away Joe's sins and to give him eternal life. The Johnson family had prayed a long time for the Wilkens family. Finally Joe was a born-again Christian. One of these days Brenda would be too.

"Thank you, Jesus," whispered Libby against Snowball's neck.

6

Trouble

LIBBY moved her fingers lovingly over the piano keys. Even the simple melody made her happy. Someday she would play in front of thousands of people. Someday people would pay a fortune just to hear Elizabeth Gail Dobbs play. By then she would have been adopted by the Johnsons so her name would be Elizabeth Gail Johnson. Mom and Dad would sit in special seats and listen to her concert. She would introduce them to the audience and tell everyone how proud she was to belong to the Johnson family.

Strong hands gripped Libby's thin shoulders. She jumped in surprise, then smiled as Chuck kissed the top of her head.

"You're doing great on the piano, Elizabeth." He sat down beside her and slid his arm around her waist. He was dressed in blue jeans and a dark blue, short-sleeved pullover shirt. His red hair was slightly mussed from running his fingers through it. "I'm proud of you."

Libby's heart pounded with pride. "Thanks, Dad." She wanted to say more, but she couldn't find the right words to express her feelings. She kissed his cheek. She could feel the stubble on his face.

"Honey, did you feed the sheep tonight?" His voice was low and very serious. Libby stiffened. She had forgotten to feed the sheep. How she wished she could lie, but she couldn't. "I forgot, Dad." She cleared her throat. "I'm sorry."

"Elizabeth, you know that being sorry doesn't get the sheep fed. It's important that they have plenty to eat. The ewes won't produce enough milk for their lambs if they don't eat. They need their food and water. It's your responsibility."

Tears stung Libby's eyes as she slowly stood up. A book slipped off the piano and plopped to the floor. Quickly she bent to pick it up and blinked away her tears. She didn't mind feeding the sheep. But now it was dark out and the yard light didn't reach the sheep pen. Her heart skipped a beat. She would not think about being afraid of the dark! "I'll feed them now." Her voice was husky and low, with sobs coming between words. "I'm sorry, Dad. I won't forget again."

"I'll send Ben out with you." Chuck stood with his thumbs looped in his pockets.

Libby wanted to sink through the floor. Ben never forgot any of his chores. Ben hardly ever got into trouble of any kind. He was such a good person. She hated for him to know she had forgotten to feed the sheep, but she dreaded going outside alone in the dark even more.

Ben met her on the back porch just as she slipped on her green-plaid jacket. She could tell by his flushed face that he was upset. Was he angry because he had to go outdoors with her?

"Will you hurry up, Libby! I can't take all night, you know." Ben jerked open the door and glared over his shoulder at Libby.

Libby stared at Ben in surprise. Was he really talking that way? She'd never heard him speak that impatiently. "What's wrong, Ben?"

"You know."

"You mean because you have to go outside with me?"

"No."

"Then what?" She followed him outside, just as he slammed the door shut. Rex ran to them, wagging his tail excitedly. Light spread around the back of the house. At the edge of the light, Libby turned on the flashlight and the beam shook as her hand trembled.

"Why'd you tell Dad that I knew you hadn't fed the sheep?" Ben grabbed her arm and stopped her.

"I didn't! I didn't even think about it." Hot tears came to her eyes. It was terrible to have Ben angry with her.

He released her and walked away in a huff.

Libby ran after him, almost falling as she stumbled over something in the yard. "Don't you believe me, Ben? Wait! Ben, please."

Ben stopped and turned toward Libby. "Dad asked me why I didn't do it myself or remind you when I saw it wasn't done."

"Did you know I'd forgotten?"

"Sure. I'm not stupid."

Libby shook her head. "But why *didn't* you remind me?" Suddenly she was angry too. "Dad's not stupid either, Ben. He probably realized you'd know if the chores were done or not." She shoved the flashlight into his hands. "Hold this while I get the hay. If you don't want to help me, then go back to the house without me." She figured he wouldn't care if she was afraid of the dark.

Ben waited while she pitched the last of the hay into the sheep pen. She was glad Ben stayed and held the light for her. Was he still angry?

Slowly they walked toward the house. "Ben, thank you for helping me. I'm sorry if I got you in trouble."

"Forget it." Suddenly Ben grabbed her arm and pulled her to a stop. "Look!" He pointed to a small, bobbing light in the driveway. "Somebody's coming."

Libby moved closer to Ben. Who would be walking to their house now? Was a stranger coming to harm them?

Brenda and Joe stepped under the gleam of the yard light. Libby sighed with relief.

"Hi," called Ben, walking toward them.

"We came to play Monopoly, if it's OK with you," said Joe, turning off his flashlight.

"Why wouldn't it be?" snapped Brenda, easing Libby out of the way so she could walk beside Ben.

"We like to play Monopoly," said Libby to

Joe. "We've tried to play with Kevin and Toby, but they're just too young. It'll be fun now."

Joe stopped Libby and waited until Brenda and Ben were at the door. "I didn't tell on Brenda," Joe said in a low voice. "But I told Mom and Dad that I'm a Christian now. Mom was mad. Dad got tears in his eyes. But they didn't say much. Brenda sure made fun of me."

"We'll keep praying for her," whispered Libby. "I'm glad you trusted in Jesus yourself."

"Me too."

"Are you two going to stand out there talking all night?" asked Brenda sharply. "We came to play a game, not to talk all night."

Libby and Joe ran to the house, laughing.

Ben pushed his flashlight into Libby's hands. "You put this away." He was still angry with her, and she still couldn't understand why.

Her hands trembled as she set the flashlight on the shelf beside the coatrack. What could she do to make Ben happy with her again?

Even as they played Monopoly, Libby tried to find ways to stop Ben's anger. Even when she "forgot" to charge him rent for landing on Park Place, he impatiently reminded her, then tossed the money at her. Libby saw the look of surprise on Susan's face. She was glad Susan didn't say anything.

When Ben walked to the kitchen for a drink of cold water, Libby followed. She waited until he set the empty glass on the counter beside the sink.

"Ben, why are you mad at me? What have I done?" She locked her fingers together until they hurt.

"Who says I'm mad?" He leaned against the counter and stared at her.

"Don't you like me anymore, Ben?" Libby's voice cracked and she thought she was going to cry. She would not cry in front of Ben!

"You're the one who doesn't like *me* anymore."

"Ben! I love you. You're my very own brother." Libby wanted to hug and kiss him, but she knew he would be embarrassed. She smiled, and finally he did too.

"Let's go finish our game," said Ben, sounding like himself again.

"And I'm going to beat you." Libby laughed happily.

They sat down, then looked at an empty chair.

"Where's Brenda?" asked Libby. She wouldn't go home without finishing the game, would she? Maybe she would if she thought Libby was going to win.

"She went upstairs to the bathroom," said Susan. "And she's been gone a long time."

Libby's heart raced. Would Brenda go into her room and see Teddy? Libby rushed upstairs. Brenda stood beside Libby's bed, holding Teddy and studying him thoughtfully.

"What are you doing in my room?" Libby firmly pulled Teddy away from Brenda. "You can't touch this bear! Get out of here right now."

Brenda flipped her long hair over her shoulder. Her dark eyes sparkled. "What are you doing with Grandma Feuder's bear? Did you steal it, welfare kid?"

"Get out, Brenda!" Libby wanted to push Brenda from her room. Grandma had wanted Teddy's hiding place kept a secret. Now Brenda knew, and she might tell everyone.

"I'm taking that bear back to Grandma. She'll be glad to see him again. Then she'll know how terrible you really are." Brenda grabbed the bear and tried to pull him away from Libby.

"You can't have it," cried Libby, shoving Brenda away and clutching Teddy to her chest.

Brenda reeled against the door, then ran downstairs, sobbing loudly.

Libby dropped Teddy on the bed and raced after Brenda.

"What's wrong?" asked Vera, taking Brenda's arm. Libby stopped near the bottom of the stairs. Vera looked sharply at Libby, then back at Brenda.

Libby's stomach flipped. She thought she was going to get sick.

"She hit me! That welfare kid hit me!" cried Brenda, sobbing harder, her hands covering her face, her shoulders shaking hard.

Libby gasped, her eyes large. She stumbled down the last step.

"Did you?" asked Vera softly, looking intently at Libby.

Libby shook her head no. She couldn't say a word. She knew everyone was looking at her.

"Brenda, I know our Libby doesn't lie. She didn't really hit you, and I don't want you lying to me again to get her in trouble." Vera sounded stern.

Brenda's tears stopped immediately. "Don't believe me if you don't want to, but she hit me and I'm going to tell my mother. And she stole Grandma Feuder's bear. I'm going to tell Grandma."

Chuck walked over to Brenda. "You will not cause Elizabeth any more trouble, Brenda. I won't permit it. If you try again, you won't be allowed in our house."

Brenda gasped, her face white. "I'm . . . I'm sorry."

Libby stared in surprise. She didn't know Brenda even knew the word *sorry*.

"We . . . we must go home right now," said Brenda, hurrying toward the door. "Come on, Joe."

"Good night, everyone," said Joe as he hastily followed his sister.

The room was quiet for a long time. Libby heard the grandfather clock tick. Out in the yard, Rex barked at Brenda and Joe. Libby looked at Vera, then at Chuck. Both of them had stood up for her. Did real parents support their own children the same way? Did they feel as if she was their real child, not just a welfare kid?

Libby flung her arms around Vera and kissed her. "I love you, Mom." Then she threw her arms around Chuck and kissed him. "I love you, Dad." Right now she felt as if she belonged to them, even though her last name was different. Maybe sharing the same last name wasn't as important as love.

Toby's Party

7

LIBBY laughed excitedly as Toby ran toward the blue van full of children from his Sunday school class. A warm breeze blew Toby's red hair into a mess. He shouted with delight as each child stepped out of the van. Rex barked happily. Goosy Poosy honked indignantly from the chicken pen. The goose didn't like being shut inside with the chickens.

"Come on, everybody; let's see the horses!" shouted Toby. He waved them toward the barn where the horses stood inside a large pen.

Toby dashed after the children, telling them not to all jump up on the board fence at once or they'd break it. Libby watched proudly as Snowball walked up to the fence and allowed the children to pet her. Snowball enjoyed all the attention and seemed to show off her beautiful white coat.

"This is a wonderful farm, Libby," said Alice Mayfield, Toby's Sunday school teacher. "I was born and raised in town, but I've always liked the country. What a great day for a party."

"I love living in the country," said Libby, smiling happily. She liked Mrs. Mayfield, who was a little older than Chuck and Vera. Her hair was chin length, almost the same style as Libby's. She was dressed in dark blue pants with a lighter blue jacket.

Ben walked from the barn, leading Sleepy, Kevin's pony. He was saddled and ready to ride.

Libby giggled as the children raced to see Sleepy. He didn't seem to be aware that they were crowding around him, admiring him. His name fit him.

"Listen up, kids," called Mrs. Mayfield. "Line up in your groups. Red team, stand here beside Libby; blue team, over there; and yellow team, by the fence." She waited patiently while the children noisily followed her directions. "OK, red team, you may ride the pony first. Blue and yellow teams, run over to Mrs. Johnson and Susan. They have games planned for you."

Libby helped keep the red team in line while they took turns riding Sleepy. Ben led the pony down the driveway, up and around the chicken coop, then back to the starting point. As each child finished a turn on Sleepy, he or she ran to join the others with Vera and Susan.

Later Susan switched places with Libby and helped the blue team ride Sleepy. Libby lined up with some kids to play games, such as Uncle Sam, May We Cross Your Mighty Dam? When someone called the color red, Libby, who was wearing a red sweater, raced across beside two little girls who were also dressed in red. She made it without being tagged! It was fun playing with little kids. Someday she'd like to teach a Sunday school class for eight-year-old children. She would tell them about Jesus and play games with them. At least Brenda Wilkens couldn't crash this party. Besides, Joe had said that they were going to their grandma's for the weekend. Libby leaned against the large maple tree to catch her breath. Without Brenda around she expected to have a wonderful time. Someone called the color blue. Libby grinned as she looked down at her blue jeans, then ran to the other base, dodging the two boys who were "it."

Later, as the children were eating around two large picnic tables behind the house, Libby sat beside a petite blonde girl with big green eyes and dimpled cheeks. Her name was Ginger. She was the prettiest little girl Libby had ever seen.

Libby bit into her hot dog. It tasted delicious. A drip of catsup ran down her chin. She wiped it away with a pink napkin.

"Are you really a welfare kid?" asked Ginger, staring at Libby.

Libby choked on the food, then nodded yes. Her heart raced and she looked around quickly to see if anyone else had heard Ginger. Suddenly, to Libby, Ginger wasn't a pretty little girl; she was ugly and mean. Libby wanted to leave the table.

"I think you're gross," said Ginger, daintily picking up a potato chip.

Libby awkwardly stepped over the picnic bench and dashed away from the table and into the house. She must not cry in front of the children. The house was quiet and stuffy. She jerked off her red sweater as she ran into her room. With a sob she flung herself across her bed and buried her face against her pillow. How she hated that little girl! She wanted to go right back out there and slap her face and make *her* cry. Or maybe she could turn Goosy Poosy loose to scare her. She would think of something to pay her back!

Libby lifted her tearstained face and sat dejectedly on her bed. Would she *ever* be like other kids? Would she spend her whole life hitting others for calling her a welfare kid? She thought of something Dad had said to her just the other day in his study.

"Elizabeth," Chuck had said earnestly while paging through his Bible on his desk, "don't try to hurt other people just because they hurt you. God wants us to show others love, even when they are unkind to us. In Luke 6:27, Jesus says you should do good to those who hate you."

Libby picked up Pinky and Teddy and hugged them both. She walked to the window and looked out at the kids below. Ginger was still at the picnic table. How could she show love to that girl? It would be easier to be mean to her.

In fact, Chuck had told her that she herself couldn't show love to a hateful person. Christ within her would show the love. Libby put the stuffed animals back on the bed. Then she bowed her head and closed her eyes. "Jesus, thank you for your love. Forgive me for thinking bad thoughts about Ginger. I'm sorry. Help me find a way to show Ginger that I love her."

By the time Libby walked back out into the warm sunlight, she was smiling and happy. She was just in time for the treasure hunt. She noticed that Ginger didn't have a partner. Libby ran to her.

"Ginger, I'll be your partner in the treasure hunt." Libby could see Ginger hesitate, then reluctantly agree. Libby managed a smile that she really meant.

Libby was surprised how easy it was to be nice to Ginger while they raced from clue to clue. Once Ginger tripped and fell. Libby helped her up and brushed the grass and dirt off her.

"You're nice," said Ginger with a puzzled frown. "I didn't think you were nice." She smiled and slipped her small hand into Libby's.

A warm feeling spread inside Libby. She knew Jesus was helping her. It was a great feeling.

When they found the treasure tied up in a lilac bush, Ginger jumped up and down with joy. "Thank you, Libby. I'm glad you helped me. Quick. Take it down and let's open it."

Ginger jumped around, making Libby laugh so hard she could hardly untie the string holding the treasure.

"You open it," said Libby, handing the package to Ginger. Libby already knew what was inside, but it was fun watching Ginger's excitement. Libby heard the others shouting as they found treasures. Vera had hidden enough prizes for everyone.

Ginger ripped off the paper and held up two prizes. "Do you want the game of tic-tac-toe or the candy bar, Libby?"

"Let me see." Libby studied them carefully. "I think I'll let you choose first. It doesn't matter to me which one I get."

"Goody! I'll take the game. My brother Tom has tic-tac-toe, but he won't let me play with his."

Libby opened the candy bar and broke it in half. "Here, Ginger. You can share my candy bar."

"Thanks, Libby." She ate it in three bites.

Libby laughed. "This is a fun day, isn't it?"

"Oh, yes! You're not gross, Libby. You're nice. I love you." Ginger threw her arms around Libby and hugged her hard.

Libby's eyes glistened with tears. "I love

you, too, Ginger. And Jesus loves you. Did you know that?"

Ginger shrugged.

"He does, Ginger. He loves you so much that he didn't want me to be mean to you even when you made me feel bad. He helped me to be kind." Libby stuffed her hands deep into her pockets. She felt strange talking like that.

Ginger tipped her head sideways and studied Libby. "If Jesus loves me, then I love him, too."

"Listen up, kids," called Alice Mayfield, clapping her hands to get their attention. "We have a special surprise for you today. Come sit in the grass over here and I'll tell you about it."

Libby followed Ginger, then stopped when she saw Adam standing by a tree. Ginger ran off to sit with the others, and Libby walked over to Adam. "Hi, Adam. I didn't know you were coming to Toby's party."

"I only came because Grandma made me. She's going to tell the kids a story or something." Adam shook his head and frowned. "She'll probably tell them one of those silly Bible stories about Jesus."

"I like to hear Grandma tell Bible stories.

And they aren't just silly stories, Adam. The Bible is God's Word." Libby couldn't understand why Adam was so touchy about Jesus and the Bible.

Grandma walked up. "How's Teddy?" she asked Libby softly. "I miss him a lot."

"He's just fine." Libby grinned. "I think he likes Pinky, my big pink dog that Susan bought me when I first came here. They sit side by side on my bed."

"No one tried to get him?" Grandma gripped Libby's hand tightly.

Libby hesitated. Brenda hadn't succeeded in taking Teddy, but she did know about his being in Libby's bedroom. Quickly Libby told what had happened when Brenda was in her room. Grandma shrugged and said it really didn't matter, just as long as she didn't take the bear.

"Now I'm going to tell a story to the children. I'll talk to you later, Elizabeth." Grandma walked over to Mrs. Mayfield and greeted her young audience.

"What did Brenda want with the bear?" asked Adam as he and Libby walked around the house. "Did she find something on the bear or inside the bear?"

Libby stopped and stared at Adam. "What

do you mean? What is there to find, Adam? Is there a mystery?"

Adam was silent for a long time. He stared at the ground, biting his lower lip. Finally he looked at Libby. "I think so."

8

Rainy Day

LIBBY curled up tighter in the blue chair in the family room. She rested her chin on her knees and closed her eyes. She couldn't get her mind off what Adam had said about Teddy yesterday. If there really was a mystery, what was it? Would she ever learn the truth? Maybe she could ask Grandma. But Grandma would have told her already if she had wanted her to know. Adam could have been wrong. Or maybe he just wanted to cause trouble again.

Libby stretched and yawned. She wouldn't think about Teddy anymore today. She looked over at the piano. Maybe practicing her music would take her mind off Adam and Grandma.

Libby sat down to play just as Toby and Kevin rushed in and looked out the window.

"Rain, rain, go away," chanted Toby. He pressed his nose against the glass.

"I hate rain," said Kevin impatiently. "I wish it would never rain again."

Libby turned from the piano and laughed. "I didn't think farm boys ever talked that way."

Chuck walked across the room and put his arms around the boys. Toby's hair was a brighter red than Chuck's. Kevin's blond hair looked almost white next to the redheads. "Come on, boys, we can't allow a Sunday afternoon to be gloomy. We'll think of something to do."

"Let's sing," said Susan, entering the family room with Mom. She was always ready to sing.

Libby jumped up from the piano. "You play, Mom, and we'll sing. I'll call Ben."

"He's in the basement putting a model together," said Kevin as he leaned against the piano. "I don't know if he'll want to sing."

"Ben has something to work out between himself and the Lord," said Chuck. "We had a long talk about it last night."

"What did you talk about?" asked Toby eagerly.

Chuck ruffled Toby's red hair. "It's a

secret. I promised him I wouldn't tell. Elizabeth, call him and we'll sing."

Libby hurried to the basement door. Ben had never kept a secret from the family, especially from her. But she'd noticed his anger toward her again last night while they cleaned up after Toby's party. Had she done something to upset him? Why wouldn't he talk to her about it? She called down to him and waited. When he didn't respond, she called again.

He scowled up at her from the bottom of the steps. "I'm coming. You don't have to yell your head off."

Libby walked back to the family room, her shoulders drooping. How could she be happy when Ben was mad at her? She felt full of unshed tears, as many as the raindrops outdoors.

Ben smelled like plastic glue when he walked into the family room and stood beside Susan at the piano. He didn't even look at Libby.

Chuck clamped his hand on Ben's shoulder and squeezed it. "We should thank God for helping us with every problem we have."

Ben looked up and a smile crept across his face. "You're right, Dad." He turned to Libby. "I'm sorry I was crabby to you."

Suddenly her inside tears were gone. "That's all right, Ben."

Chuck kissed the top of Vera's head. "We're ready to sing, honey."

Vera ran her slender fingers over the keys. The melody of a praise chorus filled the room and shut out the drum of the rain on the windows. A fire burned merrily in the fireplace at the end of the room.

As they sang a love song to Jesus, Libby wondered how she could love him more than she already did, but each day her love grew. And she was learning that Jesus really did love her. He cared about her. Chuck said Jesus loved all of them the same. She had thought Jesus would love Ben the most because he usually was so good. But Chuck had said that Jesus loved even the very worst person. Libby smiled. That must be Brenda Wilkens.

Libby stopped singing. Since Jesus loved everyone, that would mean he loved her real mother. Libby's heart skipped a beat. How could anyone love Mother? It hurt too much to think about her.

"Anything wrong?" Chuck whispered close to Libby's ear.

Libby smelled his aftershave lotion. His breath tickled her ear. She shrugged.

"We can talk later in the study," he said.

"Maybe." She didn't want to think or talk

about Mother. She forced her thoughts to return to the singing, and then she felt good again. Someday when it wouldn't hurt so much she'd think about Mother. But not today.

After a few more songs and hymns, Vera turned from the piano. "I think we're all losing our voices. We'll sing again later."

Chuck sat on the floor, and Toby and Kevin plopped down beside him. "I don't think we told Toby about how we bought this farm, did we?"

Toby leaned on Chuck's knee. "Tell me."

Libby sank down in the blue chair again and listened to Chuck, happily watching his expressive face.

"A long time ago we saw this farm. Mom and I looked it over and claimed it for ourselves. Jake Beeler owned it and wanted to sell it. We offered him a fair price, but someone else offered him more. He didn't know it, but we just knew we'd get it. When he found out the other man wanted to subdivide and sell the farm in little parcels of land with a small house on each piece of property, he turned down the offer." Chuck grinned at Vera. "Mom and I knew it was ours weeks before Jake Beeler knew."

"We walked over the entire 200 acres and dedicated them to God," said Vera.

"We wanted to use our farm to glorify the Lord." Chuck's face was thoughtful.

"You should have seen the house that once was here. That was before Ben was born." Vera pushed her blonde hair back and laughed. "That house was older than Jake Beeler, and he was 80. It had one tiny bedroom, a kitchen, a living room, and a bathroom. We knew we wanted a big family and would need a big house. We asked God to give us this house. We saw the blueprints in a magazine and sent for them."

Libby leaned forward, catching the faint scent of Vera's perfume. A log snapped in the fireplace. The wind whipped rain against the windows.

"By the time the house was built, Ben was two years old and Susan was almost a year. Then Kevin came along. We had seven bedrooms and only three children. We started praying for two more children to fill the rose and the blue bedrooms. Libby came for the rose-colored room and then Toby for the blue. The guest room, of course, we keep for grandparents or other visitors."

"We sure got tired of waiting," said Susan

with a big sigh. "I always wanted a sister, but we never got one. Then one day Libby came, and now I have a sister."

Libby's eyes smarted with tears. She blinked hard. She had been prayed into the Johnson family. She had her own room, her own horse, and she was learning to play the piano. No one had ever offered to give her piano lessons before. Best of all, she had a wonderful family who taught her about Jesus. The rainy days could come all they wanted. She was happy.

They talked and laughed for a long time. Then Libby asked, "Dad, did you know Grandma Feuder's children?"

Chuck walked to the sofa and sat down beside Vera. He took Mom's hand and held it firmly. "I met Jane and Larkin a few times, but they were already married and had children when we moved here. Their children are my age, I think. Why do you ask, Elizabeth?"

Libby hugged a blue-flowered pillow. "Grandma's been saying funny things about Henry Comstock. Did you ever meet him?"

"A couple of times. He never did get along with Grandma."

"Who's Henry Comstock?" asked Toby, rolling over on his stomach and looking up at Libby.

"Grandma's son-in-law." Libby's heart skipped a beat. "I think he's trying to do something bad to her. I don't know what, but Grandma sometimes seems scared when she talks about him." Libby saw the quick look that passed between Chuck and Vera.

"He tried to take the farm a few years back," said Chuck, shaking his head. "He said the work was too much for her; he even wanted to have her put in a nursing home. But she kept ahead of him by selling all her animals—except the dogs, cats, and chickens. She told him even an old woman can take care of chickens."

Susan pulled her knees up under her chin. "Maybe he won't try anything with Adam there."

Ben snorted. "And how would Adam stop him? Adam's no help at all."

"He is too," said Libby sharply. "You just say that because you don't like him."

"Adam doesn't like anybody except Libby," said Susan. "And sometimes he doesn't like her."

"He's a very unhappy boy," said Chuck. "He's been in my store with Grandma, and I can tell by the way he acts that something is bothering him."

Libby remembered the time she'd seen him crying and knew something was hurting him. But what?

"I think we should pray for Adam and for Grandma," said Vera, her blue eyes serious. "God knows their problems. And he knows the solutions."

Chuck held his hands out. "Come over here, kids. We'll join together and pray."

Libby sank down beside Chuck's knee, near Susan. The grandfather clock chimed four o'clock. The rain had stopped. For a minute everything was silent. Libby thought everyone could hear her heart beating. She looked at the bowed heads, thankful that her family really cared about Grandma and Adam. As Chuck started praying, Libby bowed her head and closed her eyes.

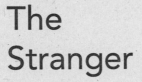

The Stranger

LIBBY walked up Grandma Feuder's driveway, humming happily. Once again it was a
warm sunny Saturday. Lapdog didn't run to
meet her. Libby supposed he was inside the
house with Grandma. A car whizzed past on
the road, then all was quiet—too quiet.

Libby walked up to Grandma's porch. She
had just lifted her fist to knock on the door
when suddenly rough hands grabbed her and
jerked her around. Libby shrieked as she
looked into the scowling face of a stranger. He
stood much taller than Chuck. He had dark
hair and dark eyes—unsmiling eyes. Even the
suit he wore was dark, along with a blue-
striped shirt and a plain navy blue tie.

"What are you doing sneaking around this
house?" asked the man in a gruff voice.

Libby tried to jerk free, but his fingers tightened until pain shot through her arm. "Ouch," she cried, swallowing hard. "I . . . I came to visit Grandma." Libby's heart thumped wildly.

"She's not home," said the stranger sharply as he let go of her arm.

"I'll find Adam and talk to him." Libby tried to sound very brave but her voice quavered.

"He's not here either. You run home, little girl, and stay away from here." He pushed her away, then grabbed her arm again. "Are you a neighbor to Mrs. Feuder?"

Libby nodded nervously. Why hadn't she called Grandma on the phone before she'd come over? Somehow she found trouble even when she wasn't looking for it.

"Then you must know what a crippled old lady Sarah Feuder is." The man pushed Libby down into the porch swing. "I want you to answer some questions for me."

Libby leaped up and tried to jump off the porch, but the man stopped her. "You aren't going anywhere until I say you can, little girl."

"I . . . I don't know anything that you'd want to know." Libby gasped in pain as the man tightened his hold on her arm.

"Do your parents provide food and help for

Sarah Feuder?" he scowled, his dark brows
almost meeting over the top of his large nose.

"Sometimes." Why would he want to know
that?

"Does your mother drive Mrs. Feuder
to town or anywhere else?" He seemed
intensely interested in Libby's reply.

Libby licked her dry lips. "Sometimes."
Who was this man? He couldn't be a friend of
Grandma's. Oh, dear! What if he was Henry
Comstock? Suddenly Libby jerked free and
leaped behind the porch swing just out of the
man's reach. Frantically she tried to find a
way to escape. Shivers ran up and down her
back.

"Has she been sick?" The man advanced
toward Libby and grabbed her again. She
screamed and kicked him hard in the shin.
"You ornery brat!" He rubbed his leg as he
cursed Libby.

She jumped off the porch, stumbled and
fell, then scrambled awkwardly to her feet.
The man ran after Libby and caught her just
as Grandma drove into the yard. Libby sagged
in relief, tears blurring her vision. Grandma
jumped out of the car and raced toward them
as fast as her old legs could carry her. Adam
followed close behind her.

"Henry Comstock, let go of that girl this minute!" Grandma shook her finger at the large man.

Libby felt his fingers loosen and she jerked free, then ran to stand behind Grandma. She was almost as tall as Grandma, but she felt safe behind this feisty little woman.

"What are you doing here, Henry? I told you never to come back." Grandma's back was straight and sparks seemed to shoot from her eyes. "Answer me, Henry Comstock!"

The big man cleared his throat nervously. He straightened his tie and stood before Grandma and Libby. Adam was standing on the other side of Libby. She was glad he was there.

"I came to talk to you, Sarah," said Henry Comstock. "I wrote to you several times and you never answered. I had to come see you. Can we go inside and talk privately?"

"Not on your life! If you want to talk, talk right here, and fast! I sure don't know what you could say to me. We've said it all before and it's settled." Grandma crossed her thin arms and waited.

Libby shivered even though the air was warmer than usual. She tugged her long-sleeved sweatshirt down over her jeans and waited anxiously. She looked at Adam and knew he was nervous too.

Henry Comstock lifted his head and stood with his hands on his hips. "I'm taking the farm, Sarah. This time you can't stop me."

"I can't?" Grandma stood with her chin high, looking younger than her years. "You can't get me off my place, Henry Comstock. You can just get in your car and leave now. Do not return."

Libby wanted to hug Grandma and protect her from this man's anger. Why couldn't the man leave Grandma alone? It was horrible of him to try and fight an elderly lady.

Henry jammed his hands into his pants pockets. "You're too old to stay on this farm by yourself."

"She's not by herself," said Adam firmly. "I'm here."

Henry Comstock laughed an ugly laugh. "I know all about you, Adam Feuder. Even Larkin couldn't handle you for long. No, I'm not worried about you, boy. I can get you to leave just as easily as I can Sarah."

Libby watched Adam's face blush a deep red. She knew he wanted to hit the man but didn't dare. She shouldn't have kicked him in the shin. Now he might try to cause trouble for the Johnsons.

Grandma put her hands on her hips and looked Henry Comstock in the eye. "Get off my place and don't come back."

"This is my farm," he said gruffly.

"It's mine until I die. Then if you want it, I can't stop you. I wish Jane hadn't written you into her will. She wouldn't have if she had known what you intended to do." Grandma moved forward and stopped just in front of Henry Comstock. "I can't fight you, Henry, but I have someone greater who can. My friend Jesus will keep you from getting this farm away from me. He cares what happens to me. He will keep you from getting this place. It's a place of love and peace. You would turn it into hate and strife."

"You're not in your right mind, Sarah. I'm going to have papers served on you, and you can't stop the law. Not even your God can stop the law once it's in action."

Libby shivered at his ugly words and clutched Grandma's icy hand. She was glad when Adam took Grandma's other hand. Could God stop the law?

Grandma laughed. "I may be smaller than you and too old to fight you fairly, but I serve a big God who can do anything. Don't challenge God, Henry, because you'll lose."

Libby smiled proudly. But the smile faded when she saw the scowl on Adam's face.

Henry Comstock stalked to his car, his back stiff, his long arms at his sides. Lapdog jumped out the open window of Grandma's car and ran after the man, barking at his heels. Henry kicked at him with a curse.

"Don't do that!" cried Libby as Lapdog ran and hid under the porch, whimpering. Forgetting her fear, Libby raced toward Henry Comstock, ready to do more than kick him in the shins, but Adam caught her arm and held her back until he drove away.

"Why did you stop me, Adam?"

"He might have hurt you."

Libby glared at Adam, her hands on her hips. "I don't care! He wants to hurt Grandma. And he tried to kick Lapdog."

"Don't worry about me or Lapdog," said Grandma with a chuckle. "We're both tough." Grandma sagged against the porch, shaking her head. "I guess I'm not as tough as I thought, though. Help me inside, Adam, and I'll catch my breath. I don't want Henry coming back and thinking he got the best of me."

"Should I call Mom to come down to be with you?" asked Libby as she and Adam helped Grandma to a chair at the kitchen table. It was Grandma's favorite chair just beside Teddy's chair. She touched his chair, then sat with her elbows on the table and her chin in her hands. Her two house dogs crowded around her feet.

"I'll be just fine, Elizabeth," said Grandma in a tired voice.

"I'll make you a cup of tea," said Adam as he picked up the teakettle. He ran water into it and put it on the burner.

"I hate Henry Comstock!" burst out Libby as she dropped onto a chair across the table from Grandma.

"Now Elizabeth," said Grandma, shaking her head sadly, "you must remember that the poor man doesn't have any happiness or inner peace. He's always striving to get more than he has, hoping that it'll make him happy. We know that only Jesus brings true happiness. With Jesus supplying our needs, we can have what we ask for and keep it in the right perspective. Poor Henry married my Jane for her money and she never knew it. Now he wants what I have, too." Grandma clicked her tongue and shook her head again.

Adam leaned against the counter, his face very serious. "*Can* he get you off the farm?"

Libby had wondered the same thing. She leaned forward in her chair, hardly daring to breathe, her fingers locked tightly together. Suddenly the room seemed too hot and crowded.

"He'll try, Adam, but I won't go," Grandma said with a sigh. "Oh, if only Bob would come. Then everything would be all right. Bob could take Teddy, and I wouldn't worry anymore about Henry Comstock."

Libby lifted startled eyes to Adam. He looked back at her with a knowing look of satisfaction. Libby could almost read his thoughts. He was thinking he'd been right about the teddy bear. There really was a mystery.

Adam sat down on Teddy's chair and leaned close to Grandma. "Why is it so important that Bob get that bear? Tell me, Grandma."

Grandma studied him for a long time, then cupped his face in her hands and kissed him on both cheeks. "I can't tell you, Adam. It's better this way."

Libby squirmed with excitement. How could she stand not knowing? Why wouldn't Grandma tell?

"Do you think Henry wants the bear?" asked Adam in a hushed voice. Libby had never seen him so serious.

Grandma hesitated, then said, "Yes, Henry wants the bear. He'd do anything to get that bear. And he must never, *never* learn that Teddy's at the Johnsons' house. Understand, Adam? You must never tell anyone."

Adam sighed deeply and lowered his eyes. "I wouldn't tell, Grandma."

"We promise," said Libby. Adam and Grandma both looked at her as if they'd forgotten she was in the room with them. Libby felt her face turn red.

"Henry has been trying to get everything from me," said Grandma. "But right now I'm too tired to think about it."

When the teakettle began to whistle, Adam jumped up and took a cup from the cupboard. "I'll pour some tea. Would you like a sandwich, too?"

"I think I would, Adam." Grandma turned to Libby. "Would you stay for lunch?"

Libby leaped to her feet. "Oh dear! Is it lunchtime? I told Mom I'd be home an hour ago! And I still have my piano lesson to practice."

"I'm so sorry that Henry frightened you," said Grandma, squeezing Libby's hand. "Try not to worry about any of this."

"I'll try."

Grandma's eyes were filled with tears. "I know God will take care of me, Elizabeth. He always has."

Libby kissed Grandma's wrinkled cheek. "I will keep praying." Libby didn't look at Adam when he snorted impatiently.

"Take good care of Teddy."

Libby's heart pounded harder. "I will."

"Don't let anyone take him out of your room until Bob Dupont comes for him." Grandma's hands trembled. "No one but Bob, Elizabeth."

Libby licked her dry lips and headed for the door. "I promise."

10

Where's Teddy?

LIBBY sat cross-legged in the middle of her bed with Teddy in her hands. The brown-and-tan bear seemed to stare intently at her with his brown button eyes. Libby looked up with a start when Susan walked in.

"Has Teddy told you his secrets yet?" asked Susan. She plopped down on the bed beside Libby, who slowly rubbed her hands along the bear's back.

"Do you think something is hidden inside him?" asked Libby.

"Let's rip him open and see!" Susan's blue eyes sparkled and her cheeks were flushed with excitement. She bounced up and down on the raspberry-colored bedspread. "Oh, Libby, we've got to find out!"

Libby hugged Teddy close and frowned at Susan. "We can't rip him open."

"He wouldn't feel it," said Susan, grinning.

"Grandma wouldn't want us to. Oh, I wish she would tell us what the mystery is." Libby held Teddy up and shook him. "Can't you talk, Teddy? Can't you tell us if you have a secret inside you?"

Susan giggled. "You'd fall right off the bed if he did start talking to you."

"So would you." Libby giggled too.

Susan picked up Pinky and held the stuffed animal up close to Teddy. "Now, Pinky, you find out Teddy's secret; then you tell us."

"Pinky can't do that," said Kevin from the doorway. He and Toby walked into the room and stood beside the bed. "Pinky would never tell a secret."

Toby touched Teddy's nose. "That bad man had better not steal Teddy! I'm glad Grandma gave him to you to keep, Libby. He's safe with us."

"I don't want Grandma to move away," said Kevin, his mouth drooping. His eyes looked sad behind his large glasses. "I love Grandma Feuder."

"She could come live with us if he makes

her leave her house," suggested Toby. He stuck his hands in his pockets. "We have a spare bedroom."

"Mom says Grandma wouldn't want to live anywhere but in her house," said Susan. "She's lived there from the time she was first married."

Libby couldn't imagine living in one place for so many years. In just 12 years she'd lived in lots of different houses.

Just then Vera walked into the room. "Did you children forget that we're going to the Bennetts' for supper tonight? Toby, do you have your bag packed to spend the night with Paul?"

Toby dashed from the room, calling excitedly that he'd be ready soon.

"Kevin, change your clothes," said Vera, tugging Kevin's blond hair playfully. "Wear school clothes, something you can't ruin. I know you'll be playing rough tonight." She turned to Libby and Susan. "You girls are fine as you are. Just run out and shut the chicken coop and see that Rex is tied up while we're gone."

Several minutes later, everyone was ready to walk out to the car. "Wait," said Toby, dropping his bag by the back door. "I forgot my Parcheesi game. I promised Paul I would bring it." He dashed away.

Chuck laughed. "You'd think he was going for a month with all the things he has to take."

"Do I have to wear a jacket, Mom?" asked Susan, tugging off her jacket. "It's too hot."

"You'll want to play outdoors, and it will be too chilly without one." Vera slid the long strap of her purse onto her shoulder. "Just carry it for now, Susan. You can put it on when you get there."

Toby came rushing back, panting and holding the game in his hands. "I'm ready," he said happily.

Rex barked as they piled into the car. One of the horses whinnied. A car with a loud muffler roared past on the road.

❀ ❀ ❀

Libby and Susan had fun playing with Kim while the boys played with the Bennett boys. Libby almost fell asleep in the car as they drove back home late.

"I think we're all going to have a hard time getting up in the morning," said Vera as the car lights stabbed through the darkness of their driveway. "I'm glad I don't have to play the piano for church tomorrow."

"By morning you'll be wide awake," said Chuck with a smile. "And you'll wish you could get at the piano instead of having to listen to Beth Smith play."

Libby thought about Sunday school and wondered if she'd have trouble with Brenda Wilkens again. Maybe Brenda would be on her best behavior in church and would just ignore her. Libby wrinkled her nose. When was Brenda ever on her best behavior?

Libby was the first to reach the back door. She turned the knob and pushed open the door.

"Hey!" cried Chuck, hurrying to the door. "How did that door get unlocked? Who was the last one out?"

Libby's heart sank. Had she left the door unlocked? She couldn't remember if she had been the last to leave, and no one else could either.

"It really doesn't matter this time," said Vera as she flipped on the family room light. "But we'll all have to be very careful in the future to lock the door. We have too many valuable things that we wouldn't want stolen."

"Like my Monopoly game and all the money from it," said Kevin, picking up his game and hugging it against his chest.

Everyone laughed. Ben punched Kevin's shoulder. "I don't think a burglar would steal that."

Libby ran her hand over the smooth finish of the piano. At least it was too big for anyone to consider stealing.

"I don't think anything's gone," said Vera with a relieved sigh.

"I don't think anyone even came in," said Chuck, pushing his red hair back. "They would have taken the coin collection off the wall for sure."

"You're right," said Vera. She turned to the children. "Hurry to bed. No fooling around. It's very late."

Kevin and Ben rushed upstairs with Susan and Libby walking slowly behind. Libby tripped and caught the banister before she fell. Her eyes ached from being so tired. She was glad no burglar had come into their house and taken anything. Now she could sleep without worrying.

In her room she wearily undressed and slipped on her long nightgown. She picked up Pinky and set him on the round pink hassock. She stopped with a frown. Something was wrong. She puffed up her pillow. Suddenly she was wide awake. Teddy was gone!

"Dad! Mom!" she cried frantically. "Come quick!" How could the bear be gone? Why would anyone steal the bear and not anything else? She covered her mouth and her eyes grew large in alarm. Someone had walked in just to take the bear.

Chuck and Vera dashed into the room. The children were close behind them. "What is it?" asked Chuck, pulling Libby close. "What scared you?"

Libby swallowed hard. "Teddy's gone. He's missing!"

"Oh, no!" cried Susan, pressing her hands to her mouth, her eyes wide.

"Are you sure?" asked Ben, looking quickly around the room and under the bed.

"He was right beside Pinky just before we left tonight," said Libby in a shaky voice.

"Henry Comstock took him," said Kevin.

"We don't know that," said Chuck, shaking his head. "How could Henry know the bear was here? No. He wouldn't know it was here."

"I bet I know," said Susan. "Who is the only person who causes trouble for Libby?"

"Brenda Wilkens!" cried Libby, dashing toward the door. Chuck caught her and held her firmly.

"It's late, Elizabeth. You can't do anything

about the bear tonight. We can't wake the Wilkens family just to ask if Brenda took the bear. I'll call first thing in the morning and find out."

"Grandma will be so upset when she finds out the bear was taken from my room." Libby blinked hard to keep from crying. "Why didn't I hide him in my closet or somewhere? I shouldn't have left him right out in the open on my bed."

Vera sank to the edge of Libby's bed. "How would Brenda know the door was unlocked? Do you think she'd come over here and try the door?"

"We don't even know for sure Brenda did it," said Ben.

Susan glared at him. "*You* are the only one who isn't sure."

"She took it all right," said Kevin, scowling. "She loves making trouble for Libby."

"There is nothing we can do tonight, so let's get to bed," said Chuck as he walked toward the door.

"But what about Teddy?" wailed Libby, locking her fingers together. "I must get him back."

"It's only a bear, a stuffed animal," said Vera as she tightened the belt of her white terry cloth robe. "I know it has sentimental value to Grandma Feuder, but it isn't as if it's worth money."

Libby caught Susan's quick look and knew she was thinking the same thing. Teddy might be worth money. He had some secret, some mystery.

Soon everyone was gone except Susan. "What are you going to do, Libby?"

Libby shook her fist. "This time Brenda has gone too far. No matter what anyone says, I'm going to punch her so hard that it'll knock her out cold. She can't do this to Grandma's teddy bear! Oh, that Brenda Wilkens!"

Susan hugged Libby hard. "I'll help you beat her up. She's mean to do this. She's always mean! I wonder if Joe knows she did it."

"He'd bring Teddy back if he knew," said Libby.

"Let's go to bed so we can be awake when Dad calls Mr. Wilkens." Susan walked to the door, then turned. "Do you want me to sleep with you tonight? Are you scared to stay alone?"

Libby shook her head. "I'll be OK. Good night, Susan."

The door closed, and Libby sat down on

the edge of her bed, her head in her hands. Tears filled her eyes. Why did bad things always happen to her? Grandma would be just sick when she learned what had happened. But maybe Brenda would give back the bear and Grandma would never have to know. Why would Brenda take the bear? Maybe she had learned the secret and wanted it for herself. Maybe she just took it to cause trouble for her and Adam. Brenda might find a way to blame Adam. Afterall, she was still very angry with him.

With a sad sigh Libby stood up and rubbed her hands down her soft flannel nightgown. She felt weary, but she couldn't possibly sleep with Teddy gone. Slowly she paced back and forth across the room, frowning in thought. Once she got Teddy back, how could she keep him safe?

The door opened and Chuck walked in. "I had a feeling you'd still be awake, Elizabeth," he said, wrapping an arm around her shoulders. "You need to rest, honey. There's nothing you can do tonight about getting that bear back."

"I know. But I feel so terrible!" Libby pressed her face against Chuck's arm. He smelled as if he'd just taken a shower.

"I know you do. It wasn't your fault that the bear was taken." He led her to the bed and pulled back the covers. "Slide in and I'll tuck you in."

She sank down on the bed, exhausted. "Will God help us find Teddy?" She wondered if it was too hard for God.

"Mom and I prayed, but I think you and I should agree together in prayer also." Chuck tucked the covers around her, then sat down on the bed. He took Libby's hand in his, closed his eyes, and quietly asked God to help them find Grandma's bear. He prayed for a good night's sleep for Libby, too.

Just before Libby drifted off to sleep she felt him lightly kiss her cheek. Then she turned on her side and slept.

Good-bye, Grandma Feuder

11

LIBBY woke with a start, surprised to see the sun shining. How *could* she have slept so soundly? She threw on some clothes and raced downstairs, almost tripping in her haste. She had to listen when Chuck called Mr. Wilkens. Before long Teddy would be safe in her bedroom again, and Grandma would never have to know that she had almost lost her bear.

Chuck was just replacing the telephone receiver when Libby rushed into the kitchen. She could tell by his face that he was perplexed.

"Won't she give Teddy back?" Libby stood

in front of Chuck, barely able to stand still. Maybe Chuck would go to Mr. Wilkens and demand that Brenda give back Teddy. Chuck could be very firm at times.

Chuck rested his hands on Libby's shoulders. "Brenda and Joe left yesterday just after lunch to spend the weekend with their grandparents. Brenda couldn't have taken the bear."

Libby's legs felt weak. She dropped down on the nearest chair and just stared at Chuck.

Vera crouched beside Libby and spoke gently. "We'll have to call and tell Grandma what happened. She's a brave woman. I don't think it will upset her as much as you think, Libby."

"It will," said Libby with a sob. "I know it will."

"We can't call her with news like this," said Chuck. "Elizabeth and I will drive to her house and tell her."

"Right now?" asked Vera, standing up. She glanced at the carton of eggs that she'd been ready to scramble.

"Yes. Tell the kids to do the chores, then go ahead and eat without us. We'll be back before church." Chuck tugged Libby to her feet and put his arm around her waist. "Don't worry, Elizabeth, Grandma won't blame you."

Libby wasn't concerned about that. She didn't want Grandma to be upset over the missing bear. But she remembered Grandma's actions toward Teddy. She knew Grandma would feel terrible.

Libby fought back the tears as Chuck drove his pickup down the road to Grandma's farm. Libby closed her eyes tightly until Chuck pulled to a stop close to the garage. A dog barked at the tires. Chickens were already scratching the dirt in their pen.

Slowly Libby climbed from the pickup and walked to the door with Chuck close beside her. The door opened before they could knock.

"Good morning, Chuck, Elizabeth," said Grandma, smiling happily. She was already dressed in her Sunday dress. Smells of coffee and pancakes floated into the open air. "Come in for coffee, Chuck. Elizabeth, I just finished making cocoa for Adam. He isn't up yet, but you're welcome to a cup. Nice and hot, with a marshmallow."

Libby couldn't talk around the hard lump in her throat.

"We can't stay for coffee, Grandma." Chuck led Grandma to her chair and helped her sit down. He sat on Teddy's chair. "I have some bad news for you."

"Grandma's hand fluttered at her throat. "What is it?"

"Your bear is missing."

Libby saw the alarm in Grandma's face as she asked how it had happened. Libby sank into a chair while Chuck explained. How could Adam be asleep in his room when such a terrible thing had happened? He should be here with Grandma.

Grandma slumped in her chair, her face almost as white as her hair. "Henry Comstock. He was back here around the place last night. I heard him talking to Adam before I could make him leave. Adam must have told him where to find Teddy."

Libby gritted her teeth. Oh, that Adam! Wait until she got her hands on him!

"Would you like me to call the police?" asked Chuck as he leaned forward, his face very serious. He had on his blue work shirt that he always wore to do chores. His blue jeans were faded and old.

"No, Chuck. No police, please." Grandma suddenly sounded like a very old woman. "I'm tired of fighting with Henry. He can have the farm now that he has Teddy. Nothing matters anymore. Adam said he was leaving Monday, so I'll go with him and stay with Larkin awhile. I won't like living in town, but I'm too tired to fight with Henry a day longer." Grandma buried her face in her hands and sobbed. "He took Bob's bear. I'll never see the bear again, and I'll never be able to prove that Henry took it."

Libby turned away, tears running down her pale cheeks. This really seemed impossible. If Grandma was ready to give up, then she was too.

"What is so important about that bear?" Chuck handed Grandma his hanky. "Please stop crying. You'll make yourself sick."

Finally Grandma lifted her face and wiped away the tears. "We won't talk about Teddy. He's gone and that's all there is to it." She turned to Libby. "I don't want you blaming yourself, Elizabeth. When Henry makes up his mind to do something, he does it. Dry your tears, girl. We can't let this get us down."

Chuck walked restlessly around the kitchen. The dogs followed, sniffing at his work shoes. "I don't understand this entire situation, but I'll not say anymore about it, if that's what you want."

"It must be that way," said Grandma

firmly. She touched Teddy's chair, then rubbed her hand across the chair's cane seat. "I've been waiting five years for Bob to come so I could give him that bear. I thought he would come soon, even yet this month."

Libby choked back a sob and clutched Grandma's wrinkled hand. "I'm sorry. You shouldn't have given the bear to me to keep for you. It's my fault for not hiding him or something. I know you must hate me."

"I don't hate you, Elizabeth. I love you. You're a dear girl. You'll grow into a fine woman." Grandma stroked Libby's pale cheek. "If I'd kept the bear, Henry would have taken it much sooner. Please, we can't talk anymore about it." She rose firmly to her feet and lifted her chin. "I put myself in God's hands a long time ago. He is able to care for me. I'll have to make new plans for a while, that's all." She managed a smile. "Who knows? I might enjoy living with Larkin. I won't have to feed the chickens or dogs. I may even like being waited on for a change."

"It won't be bad at all, Grandma," said Chuck, smiling.

As they talked, Libby caught a fast movement past the kitchen window. She excused herself and ran outdoors. Adam was just disappearing around the side of the barn.

Libby raced after him and caught up with him beside an old black walnut tree. Its branches were still bare. She caught Adam's sleeve and held on, even though he tried to jerk free. He almost pulled her off her feet.

"How could you tell, Adam? Can't you ever be nice?"

Adam stopped struggling and stared at Libby. "What are you talking about?"

"Teddy! You told Henry Comstock where to find Teddy!" Libby let go of him, but her hazel eyes flashed fire.

"I did not!" Adam glared at Libby. He stood with his feet apart, his fists doubled at his sides. Lapdog ran to stand beside him.

"Then how did he know where to find him?"

"Find who?"

"Teddy!" Why was Adam acting so stupid?

"Is Teddy gone?" Adam sounded alarmed, but Libby wondered if he was just acting.

"You know he's gone. You told Henry Comstock where to find him and he came into our house and took him. Now Grandma has to leave the farm because she can't stand staying now." Libby gasped for breath, her sides heaving. "I wish I could punch you right in the nose for that."

"Elizabeth," called Chuck. "We must hurry home now."

"I'll talk to you this afternoon, Adam Feuder."

"I can't wait, Elizabeth Gail *Dobbs*."

She knew he stressed the Dobbs to remind her that she wasn't really anybody important and didn't really belong anywhere. Her legs barely held her as she ran and climbed into the pickup beside Chuck. She wouldn't look at Adam.

Later Libby was quiet as they drove to church. The others tried to think of ways to help Grandma. But how could they think of a way? There was no way. Libby slumped in the seat, her chin almost touching her chest. Talking about it wasn't going to help. Grandma was determined to leave. Libby knew how terrible she must be feeling. Libby remembered Christmastime when she had thought she'd have to leave the Johnson farm. It had seemed as if she would die on the spot. She bit her lower lip. They all had prayed to find a way so she wouldn't have to leave. God had answered then. But would he answer for Grandma?

As Libby sat beside Susan in Sunday school class, she listened intently to everything Connie, their teacher, said. Libby liked the light green dress Connie wore. It made her look very pretty.

"I want each of you to say the Scripture verse that we'll be memorizing today," said Connie. She'd written it on the chalkboard in her bold handwriting.

Libby could only stare at the words as the others read them.

"John 14:14—'Yes, ask anything in my name, and I will do it!'"

"Read it again," said Connie.

Libby joined in with the others, her heart racing. All she had to do was ask in Jesus' name for Teddy to be found and for Grandma to be able to stay on the farm. Quietly Libby did just that. She could barely sit still. She had to tell Grandma that everything was going to be all right. She wanted to stop Grandma before she had a chance to pack anything.

"What's wrong?" whispered Susan close to Libby's ear.

"Nothing." Libby smiled brightly and Susan blinked in surprise. She wanted to tell Susan, tell everyone, how Jesus was answering Grandma's problems. Libby just knew that if she could quote John 14:14 to Grandma it would help her find the faith and courage to stay and fight Henry Comstock.

After Sunday school Connie walked over to Libby with a large bag in her hands. "Give this to your mother, will you, Libby? She needs these pans to bake cakes for the bake sale."

"Sure." Libby took the pans. "I'll take them right to the car." She turned to leave, then turned back. "I liked the Scripture verse we learned today."

"That's one of my favorites, too," said Connie as she collected her Bible and teacher's book. "See you next week."

Libby hurried outdoors to the car. She shivered as the chilly wind hit her. Some days in April were warm and sunny; others were cold and gray. Today it seemed the sun was trying to break through an overcast sky. As she turned from the car to go back into the church she gasped in surprise. Henry Comstock was walking right toward her. She wanted to run inside to safety, but she thought of Grandma and stood her ground.

"Is Sarah Feuder inside?" asked Henry Comstock gruffly. He hunched his shoulders against the brisk wind.

"Where's Grandma's bear? You took it and she wants it back!" Libby sounded very brave, but inside she was trembling with fear.

"I don't know what you're talking about, young lady." He stopped and looked closer at her. "Oh, I didn't recognize you all dressed up fancy. What's this about a bear?"

"You already know." Libby's legs were almost ready to collapse.

"I don't have time to discuss a ridiculous bear. Is Sarah Feuder inside the church?"

Libby wanted to say it wasn't any of his business. "I don't know." This time her voice was squeaky. She dashed between the cars and back into the church. Weakly she leaned against the door. She could see Grandma's white head among the people in the second row. How would she tell her that Henry Comstock was outside the church looking for her?

Chuck motioned impatiently for Libby to sit beside him. She knew she would have to stay quiet until after the service. It was hard to sit still. Time seemed to drag. Libby practiced over and over in her mind what she'd say to Grandma as soon as she could talk to her after church.

"Libby, we must get right home," said Vera as they filed out of their pew. "I'm afraid I

117

left the oven too high for the chicken I'm roasting. We don't want burned chicken for dinner."

"I need to talk to Grandma," said Libby frantically.

"You can call her right after dinner," said Vera firmly. "Or you can run down to see her."

Libby sighed impatiently as she hurried to the car. She looked around for Henry Comstock. Was that him over there beside the Bennetts' car? Maybe it was Mr. Bennett. They both were tall and had dark hair.

Libby clutched her Bible tighter. Would she be able to talk to Grandma before it was too late?

Libby
to the Rescue

LIBBY sighed with relief when Chuck announced quietly that there'd be no more discussion about Grandma's situation. He said he knew she would want it that way. Toby shifted in his seat at the table. Libby could tell Toby was bursting with curiosity, but he didn't ask any questions that he might have been thinking.

She wolfed down the roasted chicken, baked potato, corn, and tossed salad, then passed on the banana cream pie. It was her favorite dessert, but she wasn't hungry for it today. Talking with Grandma was more important.

Just as soon as the table was cleared and dishes were loaded in the dishwasher, Libby asked for permission to visit Grandma. For a minute she thought Chuck would say no, but he reluctantly agreed.

"If she seems too upset to have you around, come right back home," he said as he stretched out on the sofa to read his Bible and listen to Vera play the piano.

Kevin, Toby, and Ben were playing checkers at the game table. It was pulled close to the fireplace, where a fire crackled. Susan sat curled in the blue chair reading a book.

Libby zipped up her red spring jacket as she ran down the driveway. She turned around once to command Rex to stay, then hurried on. Cold wind whipped against her, and she wished she had worn her winter coat. The buds on the lilac bushes looked cold and afraid to open farther. Libby watched for any signs of Henry Comstock, but she was glad she didn't see him.

Breathless from her quick trip up the road, Libby knocked on Grandma's door. The dogs barked noisily from inside. She knew they were crowded around the door waiting for Grandma to open it and see who was knocking.

The door opened a crack, then wider. "Elizabeth! I'm happy you came." Grandma let her in, then closed the door. "I was just going to call you to come see me."

"I'm glad. I wanted to talk to you this morning, but I couldn't." Libby pulled off her jacket and hung it on the coat tree beside the door. Lapdog whined at her feet for attention. She patted his head, then walked across the large kitchen.

"Sit down and catch your breath. I'll get you a glass of milk and some cookies. Adam baked chocolate chip cookies last night. He wouldn't admit it, but he was quite proud of himself."

"Where's Adam now?" Libby tried to see down the hall toward the bedroom.

"He went out for a walk just a few minutes ago. I'm sure he would've stayed if he'd known you were coming." Grandma set a glass of milk and a plate of cookies on the table. She poured herself a cup of tea in a thick brown mug. "Tea tastes better in a mug," she said. Grandma sat down and motioned for Libby to take Teddy's chair. "Now, Elizabeth girl, let me tell you what I'm going to do. I think you'll agree with me that it's the best way to go."

"Wait!" Libby took a deep breath. She hunted frantically for just the right words to say. "I want to tell you the Scripture verse I learned today." She quoted the verse, then smiled in satisfaction. "I prayed, and now I'm sure Jesus will find a way for you to stay here and will help us find Teddy."

Tears formed instantly in Grandma's eyes. She wiped them away with her apron, then smiled, showing beautiful white teeth. "I was going to tell you that what I said earlier about leaving was wrong. That verse makes me feel even more sure of my decision."

Libby locked her fingers together in her lap. Was Grandma going to say she was staying?

"I put my trust in God a long time ago. If I run off like a scared rabbit now when things get a little tough, then I'm trusting in myself. Sure, I'm weak, but Christ in me is strong and he's very able to handle Henry Comstock. I think the shock of learning that Teddy was missing made me react that way." Grandma patted Libby's hand. "You and I came to the same decision. So, Elizabeth, I'm staying and that's final. I just don't know what I'll do when Henry files a court order for me to leave here, but it's in God's capable hands."

Libby hugged Grandma happily. "I wish I could do more for you. I feel so bad about Teddy."

"So do I, honey, but we don't need to worry now that we've asked God to help us find him."

Libby propped her elbows on the table and leaned her chin on her hands. "If someone lived here with you, you wouldn't have to worry about leaving, even if Henry Comstock did get a court order, would you?"

"That certainly would stop Henry's scheme." Grandma shook her head sadly. "But no one wants to live here. I thought for years that Larkin would come to his senses and move out of the city to the farm. But he says town life is for him. I can't understand that boy."

Libby hid a grin. How could Grandma call Larkin a boy when he was 60 years old?

"And my girl Jane is dead. She would have moved in here with me, but Henry didn't want to live on the same property with me. Who else is there?"

"What about Adam?" Excitement started deep inside Libby. What about Adam? He might be the answer.

"Adam is leaving tomorrow." Grandma picked up the saltshaker and studied it with care, but Libby knew her mind was on something else.

"How can Adam even think of leaving during all this trouble with Henry Comstock?"

"Don't blame the boy. He is unhappy and can't see anything but his own problem."

Libby sat very still. "What is his problem?"

Grandma sighed as she shook her head. "I don't know. If he would talk to me, I might be able to help him. But he won't talk." Grandma patted Libby's arm. "I thought for a while he would talk to you. Now I don't think so. He has his problem locked inside himself, and he won't allow anyone to know what it is."

"He doesn't want any friends." Libby pushed back her chair and stood up. "I think I'll find him and see if he will at least say good-bye to me."

"You do that. And thank you for helping me." Grandma's blue eyes sparkled with unshed tears. "You are a wonderful friend, Elizabeth. Thank you."

Libby turned quickly away as tears came to her eyes. Someone besides the Johnson family cared about her! She wanted to tell Grandma how important she was to her and how much she loved her, but the words wouldn't come out. Would she ever learn to say what she felt? She managed to mumble good-bye and left.

Libby stood outside the door gulping in the cold air until she knew she wasn't going to cry. She looked around for Adam. Chickens scratched and clucked in the pen around the chicken coop. A barn cat stood outside the barn watching her, then streaked inside. Slowly Libby walked across the yard and around the barn. She stepped on a twig. It snapped loudly in the stillness. A helicopter flew overhead, covering any other sound. Libby watched until it was out of sight.

"I suppose you're looking for me, Elizabeth Gail Dobbs."

Libby spun around to face Adam. His face was white. The redness around his eyes revealed that he'd been crying again.

He stepped closer to her, his fists doubled at his sides. "I did *not* tell Henry about the bear! He asked me about it, but I wouldn't tell him. He seems to think everything around the farm belongs to him. He doesn't want Bob to get anything, not even the bear."

Libby's heart leaped with joy to know that Adam hadn't told. But how had Henry known where to find Teddy? She smiled and touched Adam's arm. "I'm glad you didn't tell."

"How do you know I'm not lying?"

"I know." She saw the relief on his face. They walked slowly toward the board fence and leaned against it. Libby tried to think of just the right words to get Adam talking about his feelings. Nothing came to her mind.

"Why are you leaving tomorrow?" she finally asked in a rush of words.

"I don't like it here."

She could feel his tension. "Can't you stay to help Grandma? If someone stays with her, then Henry Comstock can't get her off the farm."

"I have myself to worry about."

Libby turned on him in fury. "She's your great-grandma! How can you leave her when she needs you? She let you come stay here when you didn't have anywhere else to go."

"I could've gone lots of places."

"Name one!"

He shoved his hands deep into the pockets of his coat and turned away. "I don't want to talk about it. It's none of your business."

"If your own grandpa couldn't stand to have you around, then you must have been terrible. I bet the only other place you could've gone was where you'd have to pay someone to take care of you. Or couldn't you find a place like that? Couldn't your parents even hire someone to look after you?"

Adam slapped Libby across the face. She

stumbled back and almost fell, but caught herself on the fence. She stared at him in stunned surprise. His face turned red, then deathly pale.

"I'm sorry," he whispered, turning away.

She touched her stinging cheek. "I'm sorry for saying those mean things. I shouldn't have tried to make you mad. Oh, but Adam, please think about Grandma and not yourself. She needs you right now. Can't you stay until Bob Dupont comes?"

"What if he never comes?" Adam's eyes were filled with pain as he turned back to Libby.

"Why can't you stay with Grandma forever?"

Adam's jaw tightened. "What makes you think she'd want me that long? She would get tired of me and send me away just like the others have."

Libby swallowed hard. She knew that feeling all too well. She'd lived in constant dread of being sent away before she'd come to the Johnson home. "Grandma's different, Adam. She loves you."

"So does Grandpa, but he sent me away."

"But here on the farm you have a lot of room to run or work. In the city you didn't have space. Your grandpa probably thought you'd be happier here."

Adam gripped the board fence until his knuckles were white. "You don't know anything about it. You don't know how mad he was at me."

Libby twisted the toe of her shoe in the grass until the grass was pulled up and her shoe was dirty. She ached inside for Adam. "What about your parents? Why can't you live with them?"

"They travel all the time. They're in South America now."

"Can't you stay with Grandma until they come back?"

Adam glared at Libby. "Leave me alone, will you? I can't stay here! You should understand that."

Libby was quiet for a long time. She was remembering how scared she'd been of learning to love a home only to be pushed out again and again. Was that how Adam felt now? "I . . . I want to help you, Adam."

"And just how can you do that? You can't change me."

Libby looked at him a long time. She gathered all her courage and said, "No, but God can. Dad says that only God can take someone with bad qualities and make him or her into someone good."

Adam dropped his head against his hands on the fence.

Libby heard a step behind her and turned around. She gulped in surprise. How long had Ben been standing there? "I didn't hear you, Ben."

"I just got here." He smiled at Libby, then at Adam. "I need to talk to you, Adam. It's important."

Adam shrugged. "So, talk."

"Alone." Ben seemed very determined.

"Libby can stay," said Adam firmly.

Libby wanted to stay but she wanted to please Ben, too. She hesitated. What did Ben want to say to Adam that he had to say in private?

Ben slid his hands into his jacket pockets. "Elizabeth, you won't mind going for a walk and leaving us alone, will you? I would like to talk to Adam in private. It won't take long."

Libby turned to Adam. "I'll be back later. I think I'll walk back to the little barn where I found Snowball. I like it back there."

Adam shrugged, but Libby could tell by his eyes that he was wondering what Ben could possibly want.

"See you later," said Libby as she walked away. For a minute she thought about sneaking back and listening to them, but she knew she couldn't do that. She grinned. She really was different now that she was a Christian. Before, she wouldn't have considered *not* listening. She was very happy with the new Elizabeth Gail.

Slowly she walked through the woods along the narrow path. Maybe Ben and Adam would tell her about their talk when she got back. Ben didn't look as if they would end up fighting. Chuck had said Ben was having a struggle. Did it involve Adam Feuder?

Libby stopped and looked back at the boys. They were standing beside the fence deep in conversation. How she wished she could hear them! With a resigned shrug, Libby walked deeper into the woods.

Another Stranger

LIBBY leaned against the post and studied the old barn. Grandma had told her it was built in 1897. How many people had used the barn? What were they like? Had girls her age cleaned the barn or milked cows inside it?

With a sigh, Libby straightened up. No matter how hard she tried, she couldn't get her mind off Ben and Adam for long. Birds flew off a nearby tree. A dog barked a long way off. Was it Rex?

What *were* Ben and Adam talking about?

A noise from inside the barn startled her. What was inside? This time it wasn't Snowball. Her heart raced and she couldn't seem to get her breath. Was someone hiding inside?

Was it a wild animal? She covered her mouth to keep from crying out as the door slowly opened and a man stepped out. He was dressed in faded jeans and a dark green sweatshirt with long sleeves. He wore sneakers and had a brown backpack. His hair was longer than that of most of the men she knew, and he needed a shave. The man stopped in alarm when he saw her. For a wild moment Libby thought he was going to yell at her. She was surprised when he smiled and said, "Hello. It's kind of cold today, isn't it?"

She nodded and backed up against the fence. The man was a stranger to her. Was he a bum who spent the night in Grandma's barn? He looked about 25 five years old.

Lifting his backpack off his back and leaning it against the side of the barn, he asked, "Are you a neighbor girl?"

She nodded, swallowing hard. "I live with the Johnsons." She really should run away as fast as possible. But for some reason she stood still.

"What's your name?" The man stood relaxed with his hands on his narrow hips.

Finally she was able to say, "Elizabeth, but most people call me Libby."

"Libby Johnson. Is Chuck your dad?" He rubbed his brown hair back with his hand.

She nodded. He didn't need to know she was a foster child.

"Are . . . you a stranger?" She blushed at such a silly question.

"I guess I am to you, but your dad knows me. I'm Bob Dupont."

Libby gasped and pressed harder against the fence.

"Hey, you don't have to be afraid of me. I don't hurt people." He smiled, showing bright white teeth against his tan face.

"I . . . I know who you are. Grandma has been waiting and waiting for you, but Teddy was stolen, so now she doesn't think you'll come."

The man chuckled and held out his hands. "Hey, you're going too fast for me." He leaned against the fence. "Would you please explain slowly what you're trying to tell me?"

Libby took a deep breath and locked her fingers together tightly. "Grandma Feuder told me about you. She said you bought her a teddy bear when you were 12 years old and that she promised to give him back to you."

"That bear. I don't know why Grandma keeps insisting that I want that bear back. I don't have any kids who would want to play with him." Bob Dupont rested his foot on the bottom rung of the fence, then leaned his elbow on his knee.

"Oh, she won't let anybody play with Teddy. She used to set him on a special chair where he could watch her eat. But then Henry Comstock wanted to steal him, so Grandma gave him to me to take home. Only Henry Comstock stole him anyway." Libby nervously pushed her hair back from her narrow face.

"He stole the bear from your house?" Bob stood up straight.

"Yes. Just last night, and Grandma was going to leave and live with Larkin, but she said since she trusts God, he'll take care of her. Henry can't make her leave." Libby trembled as she tried to stop talking so fast. "But if someone doesn't come to stay with Grandma, then she will have to leave. Henry Comstock says she's too old and weak to stay on the farm by herself."

"Good old Henry. Up to his old tricks again. He can sure be mean." Bob thumped his fist against his palm. "That man makes me very angry."

Libby jumped when a bird flew past her.

"I saw someone staying with Grandma. How can Henry say she's alone?"

"That's Adam, Grandma's great-grandson. But he's leaving tomorrow." Libby took a deep breath and looked right at Bob Dupont. "Can't you stay with her?"

His face grew pale. "No. I shouldn't have come now, but I had to find out if she's well."

"She needs you." Libby was surprised that she had the courage to speak up to the man.

"I need her too, but things aren't that simple." He ran his long fingers through his hair. "I didn't know Henry would be around causing trouble. I wanted to observe Grandma without her seeing me."

"But why?" cried Libby. She wanted to grab Bob by the hand and drag him to Grandma.

He shrugged, his face suddenly sad. "I saw her walk to her car this morning when she left for church. She looked great."

Libby's heart thudded so loudly she thought he would hear it. "Why didn't you talk to her? She's been waiting for you to come. She wants to talk to you. She told me she thought you'd come in April. It's April."

He rubbed the back of his hand across his eyes. "I don't think she really wants to see me. I've been promising for years to come back. And now that I'm finally here, I'm not sure I want to see her, especially if she thinks I came only for a handout."

Libby frowned. What could he mean? "Grandma wants to see you. I know she does."

He studied her intently, then sighed. His voice shook. "You really mean that, don't you? I think I'll get my backpack, and we can both walk to Grandma's home." His hands trembled as he picked up the brown backpack from against the gray barn and shifted it into place on his back.

Libby could barely keep from running as they walked along the path back to the house. Grandma would be astonished. God had answered prayer and sent Bob Dupont home. Now, if he'd answer about Teddy, all would be well.

Ben and Adam were still standing beside the fence. They were talking, and even Adam laughed happily. Libby's eyes widened. What had happened? In her excitement over Bob Dupont, she had forgotten about Adam and Ben.

"Ben and Adam, I want you to meet Bob Dupont," said Libby proudly. She laughed at their shocked expressions.

"I can't believe you're really here," said Adam, slowly walking around Bob Dupont to study him from every angle. "I've been hearing about you for a long, long time."

"Grandma will be so glad you're home," said Ben, smiling.

"I think I'll go see her right now and not put it off any longer." Bob walked purposefully toward the house with Libby and the boys close behind. No one spoke. A rooster crowed.

Bob knocked. Libby waited breathlessly, her hands clasped at her mouth. She looked at Ben and Adam. They were as anxious as she was.

Grandma opened the door, then cried out in joy as she flung her arms around Bob. He hugged and kissed her, tears sliding down his cheeks to meet with hers.

Grandma stepped back and studied him closely. "You look starved to death. Come inside this minute and talk to me while I fix you a good meal."

Bob shrugged off his backpack and propped it beside the door. He winked and smiled at Libby. "See you later, little friend."

"Did she bring you back to me?" asked Grandma, once again hugging Bob close.

"We met at the old barn in the woods," said Bob, grinning.

"Thanks for bringing my boy to me, Elizabeth."

As the door closed behind the two, Libby heard Bob explaining to Grandma how he came to be in the barn. She smiled. What a happy, happy ending for Grandma!

Ben touched Libby's arm. "Wait until you hear what we have to tell you!"

She didn't know if she could stand any more excitement. "What? What is it, Ben?"

They sat on the porch step with Libby in the middle and Ben and Adam on either side. Ben leaned forward and grinned at Adam. "You tell her, Adam."

Adam cleared his throat. He snapped a small stick in half and tossed the pieces aside. "Ben and I had a long talk, and I decided that I wanted to be a Christian like all of you. We prayed and now I am one. I know Jesus died for my sins and rose from the dead. He's my Savior."

Libby could only stare. Then she blurted out, "That's the best news ever! Quick, quick tell me about your talk and everything."

Ben smiled, then got serious. "I had to tell Adam I was sorry for being so mean to him."

Ben blushed and couldn't look at Libby. "I was jealous because you seemed to like him better than me—even when you knew he was bad all the time. But I was wrong for feeling that way. I asked Jesus to forgive me and I asked Adam, too." Ben looked at Adam and smiled. "I just knew Jesus wanted me to talk to Adam about being born again, but I was too scared. I didn't want to because I was mad about everything. But today I knew I couldn't wait any longer. Now we're friends, and Adam is a believer."

Adam smiled. "And I'm happy, Elizabeth. Now I can stop running away all the time. I do want to stay with Grandma, and I think she will want me to. Maybe I can convince my parents to move here. They will still be gone a lot, but they can be here part of the time."

Libby blinked back happy tears. "I'm glad you decided to stay, Adam. You can go to our school and our church."

Adam hesitated. "I haven't gone to school with other kids for a long time. I don't know if I could do it."

"You can," said Ben firmly. "Dad always tells us to remember that we can do everything with the help of Christ who gives us strength."

Libby felt as if she'd burst with happiness. God was taking care of everything. How wonderful it was to be able to trust him! Now all he had to do was answer the prayer about Teddy. Maybe Jesus would send Henry Comstock here with the bear in his hands. Libby giggled. Henry Comstock would look very funny carrying Teddy under his arm.

"What's so funny?" asked Ben, nudging Libby.

She jumped to her feet, her eyes sparkling. "I wish Henry Comstock would come back with Teddy, but wouldn't he look funny holding him?"

"Did you talk to Bob about the bear?" asked Adam thoughtfully.

"Yes."

"Does he know the mystery behind it?" Adam jumped up expectantly. "We might know the answer soon."

Libby shook her head. "He couldn't understand why Grandma wanted to give him the bear. If there's a secret about Teddy, Bob Dupont sure doesn't know about it."

Ben stood up and pulled his jacket down over his jeans. "Now that the bear is gone, it doesn't matter if there's a secret or if there isn't."

Lapdog barked frantically as a car turned into the driveway and came to a stop. Henry Comstock stepped confidently out of the car. Libby blinked in surprise. She had just thought of him and here he was. She really expected to see the bear, too, but his hands were empty. He strode up to them with an angry scowl on his face.

They blocked his way to the porch. "Get out of my way. I've come to talk to Sarah one last time. I don't want you kids getting in my way."

"We want the bear back," said Libby, her fists clenched at her sides. "We want it back right now."

Henry Comstock looked down his large nose at her. "You are as crazy as that old woman inside." He tried to walk around them, but Ben jumped in his way. Henry looked down at Ben. "You're asking for trouble, sonny."

"Grandma doesn't want you here," said Ben. His red hair looked even redder as the sun slid from behind a cloud and shone brightly.

Lapdog sniffed Henry Comstock's shoes, then whimpered and ran under the porch. Libby knew he was remembering when the man had tried to kick him.

"You kids are going to get hurt if you don't move this minute." He scowled at them fiercely. "Sarah Feuder knows I have her beat this time."

Adam lifted his chin and looked Henry Comstock in the eyes. "Your plan didn't work, and it won't work. I am going to stay with her from now on. I'm sure my parents will be moving in too. I'll do the chores and help Grandma with everything. She won't be alone ever again."

Henry cursed, then shoved Adam and Ben out of the way. He strode up the porch steps and pounded on the door. The dog inside yapped loudly.

Libby waited anxiously for Grandma to open the door. Libby wished she were big enough to stop Henry Comstock from being here. Maybe if the three of them grabbed Henry, they could drag him back to his car.

The door opened, and Grandma stood face-to-face with Henry Comstock.

Teddy's Secret

LIBBY gasped. She wanted to find a way to protect Grandma from the mean man.

"What are you doing here again, Henry?" asked Grandma, frowning.

"Henry Comstock is here?" Bob Dupont stepped through the door and looked into Henry's surprised face.

Henry backed up, his face a sickly gray. "What are you doing here?"

Grandma smiled. "He came home, just as I knew he would."

Bob grabbed Henry's jacket lapels. "What's this I hear about your sneaking into the Johnsons' house?"

Henry tried to break free. His face darkened. "I was never in the Johnsons' house. I don't know why you say that."

143

"Drop the pretense, Henry," said Bob impatiently. "Grandma wants that bear back right now! Is it in your car? Did you destroy it?"

"You are all crazy. Turn me loose this minute, Bob. I could cause a lot of trouble for you, and you know it." Henry struggled and finally jerked free.

"It would be wise for you to leave and never return," said Bob. "Leave Grandma alone."

"I'm not beat yet. One of these days she'll die, and this farm will be mine; you won't get one tiny part of it."

Bob chuckled. "That's fine with me. I have a business of my own, and I don't need to live off old ladies."

Henry choked with rage. He turned and strode to his car. With tires squealing he drove away.

Libby watched the relief on Grandma's face. Grandma hugged Bob and smiled at everyone.

"I'll stay with you, Grandma, if you want me," said Adam happily. "And guess what? Ben helped me to accept Jesus as my Savior."

Grandma hugged and kissed Adam, tears of joy running down her wrinkled cheeks. "I'm happy for you *and* for me. I love having you here. Besides, who can make chocolate chip cookies as well as you?"

Adam blushed and looked quickly at Libby. She smiled.

"Elizabeth, I believe Chuck and Vera would like to hear all the good news." Grandma pulled the door shut. "We'll ride over in my car and give them a big, wonderful surprise."

Minutes later Libby walked proudly into the family room with Grandma, Bob, Adam, and Ben close behind. Music from the CD player filled the room. Toby had just scored a point in a game he was playing and was shouting in triumph.

"Look who came to visit," said Libby, stopping in front of the sofa where Chuck and Vera sat reading. Libby laughed at the surprised then happy looks on their faces. Libby stepped back as Chuck and Vera jumped to their feet.

"Bob Dupont!" cried Chuck, vigorously shaking Bob's hand.

Vera caught his hand and shook it after Chuck. "We are so glad to see you!"

"Please, have a seat," said Chuck, motioning to the sofa.

Bob and Grandma sat together, with Grandma keeping a tight hold on Bob's hand. The fire snapped cheerfully in the fireplace. "Libby found Bob in my old barn and convinced him that I really wanted to see him," said Grandma.

"You have a fine girl," said Bob, winking at Libby.

She was glad he didn't know she was only a foster child. That might spoil everything. She blushed and looked down at her feet.

Susan laughed and sat on the carpet beside Libby. "Why do all the exciting things happen to you?"

"Probably because she doesn't stay home with her nose buried in a book," teased Chuck with a grin. He turned to Grandma. "I believe we have seen a prayer answered today, haven't we?"

"More than one," said Grandma.

Libby listened happily as Grandma talked. It felt wonderful to hear someone saying good things about her for once. But she grew tense when the teddy bear was mentioned. That wasn't good at all. If only she had taken better care of Teddy!

"I believe Teddy will be found," said Grandma firmly. "God has answered other requests and he will answer this one."

"Teddy? Teddy isn't lost," said Toby.

"You were gone when it happened," said Kevin, pushing his glasses in place. "Teddy's been missing since we came home from the Bennetts' last night."

"Teddy isn't lost," insisted Toby, jumping to his feet. "I know where he is."

Libby caught Toby's arm. "He isn't there now, Toby. Somebody took him. We think Henry Comstock came in and stole him."

Toby tugged free. "I'll go see." He ran from the room and thudded up the stairs.

Vera shook her head sadly. "He was spending the night with Paul Bennett when we discovered the bear missing, so he will have to see for himself. I am so sorry about the bear. I just wish we hadn't forgotten to lock the door."

"Why is the bear so important, Grandma?" asked Bob, squeezing Grandma's hand.

Libby held her breath and waited for an answer. She looked at Adam and knew he was as anxious as she was.

"The bear has sentimental value," said Grandma softly. "But to you, Bob, it has much more."

"What?" he said with a puzzled look.

"I hate to say it now that he's gone. It

almost makes me sick to think about it. I know I should have put them in the bank, but I didn't dare because of Henry."

Libby grabbed Susan's hand and squeezed it until she yelped with pain. "Sorry," whispered Libby.

Toby dashed into the room, his cheeks flushed. "Here's Teddy." He proudly held up the brown-and-tan bear, whose button eyes seemed to take in the situation.

Libby almost fell over in surprise. She saw the amazement on Grandma's face.

"Where was he?" asked Adam and Ben together.

"I had him," he said.

Susan glared at Toby. "What made you do such a crazy thing, Toby?"

Chuck pulled Toby into his arms. "Toby, it's all right. We're glad you have the bear. Tell us how it all happened."

Toby handed the bear to Grandma, then looked at Chuck. "When we were going to the Bennetts', I ran upstairs to get my Parcheesi game. I thought about Teddy sitting in plain sight on Libby's bed. I knew if Henry Comstock got into the house he would find him and take him. So I . . . hid Teddy in a box under my bed."

"Oh, Toby!" cried Libby joyfully.

"Thank you, Toby," said Grandma, smiling through her tears. "And thank God for another answer." Grandma looked down at Libby. "Elizabeth, find me a pair of sharp, pointed scissors and bring them here. I'll show all of you Teddy's secret."

Libby's legs trembled as she went to the kitchen for the scissors. She returned to the family room and reluctantly handed the scissors to Grandma. "You won't hurt Teddy, will you?"

"He's not real, Libby," said Susan, shaking her head.

"Sometimes he seemed real to me," said Grandma as she carefully laid Teddy on her lap. "I won't hurt him, Elizabeth. Nothing will hurt him now. He has kept his secret long enough."

What was the secret inside Teddy? Libby watched as Grandma carefully clipped the seam down Teddy's middle. She lifted out a small white sack and handed it to Bob Dupont.

"Grandpa and I wanted you to have the contents of this sack," she said softly. "We wanted them for your mother, but when she married Henry and he . . . well, you know

Henry . . . we decided to keep them a secret and save them for you. After Grandpa died and Henry really started causing trouble for me, I sewed the bag into Teddy's stomach. He has kept the secret well for a long time."

Libby leaned forward as Bob slowly opened the bag. Everyone was so quiet that she could hear the fire crackling in the fireplace.

Bob poured coins into his hands. Tears filled his eyes. "These are old coins, aren't they?"

"Yes. Grandpa bought them as an investment. They are yours. I know a man who would give you good money for them tomorrow if you want to sell them."

Bob cleared his throat and wiped the tears away with the back of his hand. "I'm not much into old coins, but I'm sure they are worth a lot of money, and money is what I need right now."

"Mom knows a lot about old coins," said Kevin, wide-eyed. "Don't you, Mom?"

"Quite a lot," said Vera, smiling. "I have several books that will help you find the value of the coins, Bob."

Bob handed the coins to Vera. "Check them over for me and tell me what you think."

Libby and the others crowded around Vera, causing her to almost drop the money. She laughed good-naturedly. "Kids, I know you're all excited, but please stand back a little. We'll spread the coins on the table and then you can all see them."

Bob stood up and walked with Vera to the table.

Libby looked at Grandma's proud face. "I can get a needle and thread so you can sew Teddy back up." She smiled at Grandma. "I'm glad Teddy had such a good secret inside him. I tried to get him to whisper it to me, but he wouldn't."

"I thought you might guess he had something inside him, but I knew I could trust you." Grandma wiped tears from her faded blue eyes. "Get the needle and thread, please, Elizabeth."

Later Libby sat beside Grandma on the sofa while Grandma finished sewing Teddy's seam shut again. The others were in the dining room crowded around the table.

"He's as good as new," said Grandma, holding Teddy in front of her. "My kitchen will not seem the same without Teddy."

Libby laughed. "Are you sure Bob wants to take him home with him? I think he's too old to play with a teddy bear."

"He can save him for his children when he

marries." Grandma propped Teddy on the couch and slowly stood to her feet. "Elizabeth, I want you to remember always to trust God. He has answered our prayers in many ways. Every day I realize how important trust is. I do want you to learn this while you're still young."

Libby nodded. "I am learning, Grandma. I'm glad I can love and trust Jesus." She paused. "I've never said this before, but trusting anyone has been very hard for me. Yet when I think that Jesus really does love me and will answer my prayers, I know I can trust him."

Grandma hugged Libby close. She smelled like peppermint candy. "I love you, Elizabeth Gail. I'm proud that you're my friend."

"Hey, let me hug Libby too," said Bob from behind them. "I'm proud to have her as my friend. And you, too, Grandma."

Libby giggled as Bob put his arms around both Libby and Grandma. He smelled like leather. Libby's head reached to the middle of his chest. "I'm glad you have the money from Teddy," she said.

Bob walked to the couch with Libby and Grandma. He sat down with one on each side of him. Libby picked up a blue-flowered

pillow and hugged it close. "Now I can tell
you how God answered *my* prayer," said Bob
as he picked up Teddy and absently rubbed
the bear's fur. "I started my own farm, and
this year I badly needed new equipment, but
I couldn't afford it. When I asked for financial
help from God, nothing came. I knew if I
could see Grandma, maybe even talk to her,
she would encourage me to trust God and
wait to see how he would answer my prayer."
Bob cleared his throat. "With these coins God
has answered my financial need. In fact, I can
give some of the money back to God and still
have extra left over."

Libby felt the tears slide down her cheeks,
but she didn't care. They were tears of
joy.

Grandma patted Bob's knee. "I'm glad God
has answered this way. I think I'd like to see
that farm of yours."

"You're more than welcome to see it—and
to stay as long as you like."

Grandma looked across the room at Adam.
"Adam, come here a minute." She waited
until he stood in front of her. "How would
you like to go with me to Bob's farm for the
rest of the spring and summer?"

Adam smiled happily. "Do you really want

me to? Are you sure I wouldn't be in the way?"

"We both want you," said Bob. "And if Grandma's not careful, I just might keep you for good."

Libby watched Adam smile and knew he was ready to burst with pride. She knew how wonderful it felt to be wanted and loved. She lifted Teddy off Bob's lap and hugged him close. Over Teddy's head she studied her family. They were listening with interest as Bob talked. Someday she would find the most perfect way possible to show them how much she loved them.

Later, as Grandma, Bob, and Adam stood at the door saying one last good-night, Bob pressed Teddy into Libby's arms.

"I want you to have him," said Bob softly. "It's our way of saying thank you. Every time you look at Teddy you can remember the joy you helped bring us."

Libby hugged Teddy close. "Thank you," she whispered. She wanted to say so much more but she couldn't find the right words. She looked down at Teddy and smiled. His secret was gone, but he would remind her always of her new friends and answered prayers.

ABOUT THE AUTHOR

Hilda Stahl was born and raised in the Nebraska sandhills. As a young teen, she realized she needed a personal relationship with God, so she accepted Christ into her life. She attended a Bible college, where she met her husband, Norman. They raised their seven children in Michigan, where she lived until her death in 1993.

When Hilda was a young mother with three children, she saw an ad in a magazine for a correspondence course in writing. She took the test, passed it, and soon fell in love with writing. She wrote whenever she had free time, and she eventually began to sell what she wrote.

The first Elizabeth Gail book, *The Mystery at the Johnson Farm*, was made into a movie in 1989. It was a real dream come true for Hilda. She wanted her books and their message of God's love and power to reach and help people all over the world. Hilda's writing centered on the truth that, no matter what we may experience or face in life, Christ is always the answer.

Elizabeth Gail Series

1. Elizabeth Gail Mystery at Johnson Farm
2. Elizabeth Gail The Secret Box
3. Elizabeth Gail The Disappearance
4. Elizabeth Gail The Dangerous Double

COMING FALL 2001

5. Elizabeth Gail Secret of the Gold Charm
6. Elizabeth Gail The Fugitive
7. Elizabeth Gail Trouble at Sandhill Ranch
8. Elizabeth Gail Mystery of the Hidden Key

COMING SPRING 2002

9. Elizabeth Gail The Uninvited Guests
10. Elizabeth Gail The Unexpected Letter
11. Elizabeth Gail Hiding Out
12. Elizabeth Gail Trouble from the Past